PENGUIN BOOKS
Holy Days

Joy Cowley lives with her husband Terry in the Marlborough
Sounds along with eight cats and seventy sheep. Her first adult novel
for many years, *Classical Music*, was published recently to much
acclaim and was shortlisted for the Montana book awards. She is
one of New Zealand's most loved children's writers and a frequent
award winner.

ACKNOWLEDGEMENTS

With gratitude to Kynan Gentry and the Business Information Service of Wellington Central Library for 1980s research.

Special thanks to Joan McFetridge for her wisdom and reassurance.

Holy Days

Joy Cowley

PENGUIN BOOKS

PENGUIN BOOKS

Penguin Books (NZ) Ltd, cnr Rosedale and Airborne Roads, Albany,
Auckland 1310, New Zealand
Penguin Books Ltd, 27 Wrights Lane, London W8 5TZ, England
Penguin Putnam Inc, 375 Hudson Street, New York, NY 10014, United States
Penguin Books Australia Ltd, 487 Maroondah Highway, Ringwood, Australia 3134
Penguin Books Canada Ltd, 10 Alcorn Avenue, Toronto, Ontario, Canada M4V 3B2
Penguin Books (South Africa) Pty Ltd, 5 Watkins Street, Denver Ext 4, 2094,
South Africa
Penguin Books India (P) Ltd, 11, Community Centre, Panchsheel Park,
New Delhi 110 017, India

Penguin Books Ltd, Registered Offices: Harmondsworth, Middlesex, England

First published by Penguin Books (NZ) Ltd, 2000
1 3 5 7 9 10 8 6 4 2
Copyright © Joy Cowley, 2001

The right of Joy Cowley to be identified as the author of this work
in terms of section 96 of the Copyright Act 1994 is hereby asserted.

Designed by Mary Egan
Typeset by Egan-Reid Ltd, Auckland
Printed in Australia by Australian Print Group, Maryborough

ISBN 0 14 100416 9

www.penguin.co.nz

In memory of my dear mother,
Cassia Summers

CHAPTER ONE

HE SAW A DIFFERENT WOMAN THIS TIME, GOTHIC AND birdlike, black hair and clothes, black lipstick, black-rimmed eyes that seemed to have travelled from innocence to knowledge to boredom in less than twenty-five years. Or maybe she was older than that. It was hard to tell. He was sure that he was a few years her senior but her lack of concern made him feel like a begging child and for that he disliked both her and himself. She wore a considerable amount of silver jewellery and she smoked, which meant that they had to move out of the staffroom to the garden seat at the end of the tennis courts where they were watched by wide-eyed students changing classes.

A group of year ten girls walked deliberately close with notepads held to their faces like fans, and he knew that a rumour would be through the entire school by lunchtime, gossip harmless enough compared with the reason for the woman's visit. The package on her lap was his script for the film story, work which had devoured so much of his summer vacation that he and Jude had needed to cancel a camping trip with the children, a sacrifice made tolerable by the prospect of extra income. They hadn't questioned the story's success. A few hours earlier, Jude had hugged him at the front door and told him it was brilliant, and she could already see his name in the credits.

Pride goes before a fall, Sister Agnes once said as she picked him up in a tangle of roller skates. Actually, the quote was *Pride goes before destruction and a haughty spirit before a fall*, but the nuns had done to Scripture the clever things that they'd done to their tattered old Edmonds recipe book. Pride before a fall, and all three Sisters encouraging him to skate on their beautiful polished linoleum, exactly as he'd described it in the script. Weeks of writing, and it wasn't only Jude who'd been sure. After yesterday's call from Waitui Films, requesting a meeting at his school, he and Jude had celebrated with a bottle of reserve chardonnay. In the fragrance of wine, his head had fast-forwarded to screenplay development and a list of actors who might be suitable to play the elderly Sisters of St Joseph the Labourer. Well, so much for that.

Her name was Susan, this woman in black who blew spirals of smoke over the dahlias by the garden seat and who turned her black-framed eyes on him without as much as a smile of apology. He gained some satisfaction from remembering her name, that sin of pride again, each time she called him Colin.

'It won't work, Colin. There isn't a story.'

'It's what happened, Susan. It's fact. Naturally I've reconstructed dialogue but I've been true to the actual events. One doesn't invent the script of a documentary film.'

'Docu-drama,' she said, tapping her cigarette over the back of the seat.

'Of course.' He saw an earwig on a dahlia leaf arch its tail like a little scorpion and wondered if fag ash contained enough nicotine to kill insects.

'You were eight years old. Little Colin O'Brien.' She picked up the thick yellow envelope. 'The perception of a child who's been taught to place nuns on a pedestal. Oh, come on, Colin! How can you say this is what actually happened. How can any eight-year-old be objective?'

'There's no such thing as an objective view, Susan. It's all perception. Yours. Mine. The producer's. The difference is, I was there.'

Another group of staring students sauntered past the tennis courts and he avoided eye contact. 'I spoke to your director, Meredith Young, herself. Her instructions were explicit. I was to write it as I remembered it, the point of view of an eight-year-old boy – which you now say is invalid.'

'What I'm saying, Colin, is we don't have a story.'

'No, Susan.' He pronounced her name with all gentleness. 'What you're saying is you don't have a scandal.'

'No scandal? In 1980 three nuns embezzle church property, abduct a child and take off. One of them dies in suspicious circumstances and the story hits the headlines like a thunderbolt. No scandal? It should have been the scandal of the year. But then, surprise, surprise, it was all hushed up.'

'Nothing was hushed up, I assure you. The only scandal belonged with the paper. It published a highly coloured, knee-jerk account that was about as far from the truth as you could possibly get. That's what I told Meredith Young and that's why she asked me –'

'Why didn't the Catholic Church object? Huh? Isn't it interesting that the paper never printed a retraction?'

He smiled and shook his head.

'You understand,' she said, patting the envelope, 'that this can't possibly work. *The Ones that Got Away* will be a TV series about crimes and scams that were never successfully brought to justice. A drunken diplomat drives on the wrong side of the road, kills three people and claims diplomatic immunity. A woman who stabs her husband after an argument about her lover gets off on a legal technicality. There's a painter who signs the name of a famous artist. When he's caught, it's discovered he's changed his name by deed poll so the signature is no longer a forgery. And so on and so forth. Tell me, Colin, where does your perception fit into this?'

'It doesn't, Susan. I made that abundantly clear to Meredith

9

Young but she told me to write the story anyway. What did she expect?' He was aware that he was talking loudly and holding his hands out to her, like a beggar. 'A work of fiction?'

She shrugged, shoulders rising as thin as a bird's wings. 'It's not a story. It doesn't fit.'

He folded his arms. 'I'm sorry but I did my best. I can't rewrite history to accommodate your particular needs. This is the truth. It's what happened and there was no crime, just a holiday.'

'Well, at least you understand why we can't use it.' She rubbed her cigarette out on the back of the seat and fired it like a small dart into the garden. 'Oh. Meredith said to tell you. She said she enjoyed it even though it wasn't what we wanted. She said it was vivid and – what was the other word? She wanted to know if you ever thought of taking up writing.'

He smiled. 'My work is writing. I'm an English teacher. I write poetry on the side.'

'Had any published?'

'A little.'

'Under your own name?'

'Yes,' he said. 'Brian Collins.'

That pushed her pause button. For a second or two she was still, then she glanced down at the name on the envelope. 'I've been calling you Colin O'Brien.'

'These Irish names are all alike,' he said.

She didn't pick up the excuse, nor did she offer an apology. She placed the package on the seat between them, stood, smoothing the tight skirt over her flat buttocks, and slung her bag over her shoulder. 'I expect you've got a class to go to,' she said, dismissing herself.

He escorted her to her car and came back to the garden seat for the ten minutes before the lunch bell, to process the conversation and analyse his feelings. He always did this, had post-mortems in which he dissected whole conversations and events, laying the separate parts out like cards on a table. Jude, who was always most serious when teasing, told him he had psychotherapy sessions with mirrors. In the old days, Sister Luke might have made some vague comment about setting fire to the tails of demons. Whatever the metaphor, the process was valid and valuable. The naming of negative energy was a way of distancing it to the point where it could be desensitised, controlled and made useful.

He knew that some of his tension was born of disappointment. He and Jude had planned painting the house with the money he got from the script. The rest concerned the tiny woman in black who was not unattractive in her thin, birdlike way, but while she had seemed physically frail, she'd had the intimidating strength of complete indifference. He'd been wounded by it in a way that was out of all proportion to the meeting. He didn't know what made her tick. That was it. The popular English teacher who worked with young women every day, who knew all the right paths in the maze of teacher/student relationships, had failed to make contact. What was behind that flat blue gaze? What did she think of him? He didn't know and he had to leave his unease undigested. Offer it up to God, Sister Agnes would have said, but he preferred to let his feelings compost into poetry, which was perhaps the same thing. He remembered Shaw's quote: 'The worst sin to our fellow creatures is not to hate them but to be indifferent to them', and he wondered if George Bernard had also met a fledgling Gorgon who had stared at him with ancient eyes turning his stomach to stone.

But he was exaggerating, a fine quality for a poet but not a teacher. For a moment he put his head back, face to the sun, and closed his eyes.

Script rejected. Six weeks of work down the tube.

Oh well, oh hell, oh ding-dong-bell.

Something fell on his hand. It was an earwig. He let it walk across the scrubland of hair below his knuckles then he put his arm over the seat and shook it into a flower.

He liked the smell of dahlias. Yes, he did, he did. It was the satisfying scent of unmade beds, of deodorant at the point of breaking down against underarm pheromones. It was a wet smell which reminded him of Jude in from her morning run, head bent over the coffee machine, the back of her T-shirt dark with sweat, neck shining and stuck with dark curls, reminded him of the taste of salt as he leaned over her to kiss the knobbly vertebra at the junction of her shoulders.

'Mr Collins?' It was Tracey Mahoney fidgeting questions with her hair and her tennis racquet. 'Mr Collins, wasn't that Susie Middleton from television?'

He shaded his eyes with his hand. 'I believe so.'

'Wow! Awesome! Do you know her?'

'No, Tracey. I've only just met her.'

'Is she going to do a film about our school?'

He stood, tucking the envelope under his arm. 'No.'

The fourth former turned away and then looked back at him, sweet-faced and sly-eyed. 'What was she here for, Mr Collins?'

He was about to tell her to run along and mind her own business, but realised that would have only fuelled gossip. 'Research,' he said. 'Old stuff that happened before you or she were born.'

'Oh,' she said, and ran off, disappointed.

The lunch bell rang, shattering sunlight and sending birds into shrill alarm. He took the envelope from under his arm and walked along the path, slapping it against his thigh until it hurt.

He would have to go to the office and phone Jude.

CHAPTER TWO

THE BOY STANDS ON THE PEDALS TO GET EXTRA PUSH FOR THE convent hill but the bike is his Dad's, big and no gears, and he gets up the slope only as far as the church, which he takes to be a sign of divine judgement. He leans the bike over to put a foot on the ground, looks up at the bricks and crosses himself before walking the rest of the way, pushing the old machine which should have gone to the dump years ago except his Dad can never bear to throw anything away.

He feels the church at his back and thinks he'll go in later when he's done his penance, adding an extra Our Father for committing sin to get the penance, something he doesn't tell the holy nuns or even Father Friel. He reckons God will understand and if he doesn't, then Mum will explain it, since she's up there, watching out for her Brian. With all the watching, he hopes she doesn't see the carry-on between his Dad and that Liz from the home appliance store. It would break her heart, that would. Did people get broken hearts in heaven?

The gate at the top of the hill is closed. He has to lean the bike against it and stand on the pedals to reach over the top to the catch, which his Dad repaired only last week. It still doesn't work properly but Dad said that was because the whole gate was euchred and no one was interested in getting a new one for the Sisters.

'It's a bloody shame,' Dad said. 'All those years working for the parish and now no one'll get off their fat arses to lend them a hand.'

The catch suddenly opens and so does the gate, and he is quick to jump away from the falling bike. He picks it up, pushes it through and lies it down again so that he can close the gate to the street. It's like a different planet inside the convent grounds, even smells different, as though all the normal old town smells have been washed in holy water or something to take the pong out of them.

He's tried explaining that to his sister Beth but she doesn't understand on account of her having a permanently blocked nose and a bad mood to match. 'You're a little greaser, Brian,' she said. 'Grease, grease, grease. You trying to be a saint or something?'

Actually, he was, but he still punched her for saying it.

That time, he had to weed the convent garden on the side of the path. It was a boring job except that under the lavender bushes there were snails that he could put in an old tin with a lid. Sister Mary Clare said it wasn't right to stand on snails but it was okay for him to take them home to feed Dad's chooks, that being natural for both chooks and snails and good for the garden.

The time before that, he'd washed jam jars in the laundry tub and Sister Agnes had given him a spoon to finish a half pot of lemon honey. He was not sure if that counted as penance but Father Friel said it was all right because Sister Agnes's lemon honey would take paint off walls, God bless her.

He leaves the bike against the back of the convent and stands on his toes to push the door buzzer. There is a wind coming up off the sea bringing a faint smell of brown kelp and sea urchins to the holy water grounds. Brian takes in a whole big breath of it. He likes smells. His Dad said he should have been a dog, always sniffing at things. He especially likes stinky smells, like farts and drains and the electric kettle just blown its element; but the only stinky smell he'd ever found at the convent was a whiff of burnt toast in the kitchen curtains.

Sister Agnes opens the door. 'Well, Brian Collins?'

She's the mother superior and she's seventy-six. He knows her age because she's also his father's aunt, and his great-aunt, except he realises that being a relation doesn't count because holy nuns have given up their families for God.

'What have you done this time?'

He stands straight, his hands at his sides. 'Blasphemery, Sister.'

'You mean blasphemy.'

'Yes, Sister. I took the Holy Name in vain.'

'What did you say, Brian Collins?'

'It was that woman, Sister, that Liz. She was making coffee and she went to the china cabinet and got out Mum's best tea-set as though she owned the place –'

'He who excuses himself, accuses himself.' Sister Agnes tucks her hands into the sleeves of her grey habit. 'What was it you said?'

He lowers his head. 'Jesus jumping Christ.'

There is silence. He looks up and sees the frown lines above her glasses. 'I am very sorry to hear that.'

'Yes, Sister.'

'You know the commandments, don't you? The Lord will not hold him guiltless who takes his name in vain.'

'Yes, Sister.'

'Your dear mother, how do you think she feels when this desecration of the Holy Name drifts up to heaven and she recognises her own son's voice. Do you think she's proud of you, Brian?'

'No, Sister.' His face gets red and he wants to tell her to leave his mother out of it. Heck, it wasn't all that terrible. Jesus jumped, didn't he? He must have when he was a kid unless he floated like an angel. The words had been carefully chosen to cause the least offence to anyone except that Liz woman who'd started making up to his father before they'd even got the headstone on his mother's grave.

'You've been in an awful lot of trouble lately,' says Sister Agnes. 'I know you miss your Mum, Brian, but you're old enough to know better.'

'Yes, Sister.'

'Have you thought your dear mother might want Elizabeth to use her tea-set? As a thank-you to her for coming in every weekend to clean the house? A widower with five young ones has to have help. Wouldn't it be the right thing to show a little gratitude, yourself?'

'She's got her claws into him,' he says.

'Who told you that?'

The boy shrugs. It was his oldest sister, Kathy, but he's not telling tales. Head down, he stares at Sister Agnes's feet, the grey woolly socks wrinkling out of the brown sandals, the hem of her skirt as frayed as the cuffs on his father's trousers. Dad said it was a decent thing to see a nun in a habit when most of them were into short skirts, showing off how worldly they were. When Brian was young, his Dad had said that nuns' legs only went up to their knees. Brian believed it and wondered how they walked. He tried tying his knees together but it was awfully hard and he was glad when Dad told him it was a just a joke.

'As I see it, there are at least two sins here,' says Sister Agnes. 'Misuse of the Holy Name and uncharitable thoughts about Miss Elizabeth Fletcher.'

'Yes, Sister.' Now he looks up at her. 'Dad says I need a big penance.'

'Are you truly sorry, Brian?'

He nods.

Her hands come out of her sleeves and she touches his shoulder. 'You can clean the guttering on the garage. You know where the ladder is. I'll get you a little trowel and a bucket.'

* * *

The nuns haven't had a car for as long as Brian can remember. His mother said that Sister Agnes had driven her Morris Minor into the back of a milk truck in the days when there were bottles, and they didn't have insurance, so after that they walked or went on buses.

The convent garage is used to store stuff for the St John Chrysostem Youth Centre down the road. Through the cobwebbed window, he sees canoes on the floor and a ping-pong table propped against the wall.

Sister Mary Clare brings the ladder to him, swaying and puffing with the weight of it, and she holds it against the wall while he climbs to the roof with the bucket over one arm.

'You'll be walking careful up there, Brian,' Sister Mary Clare says. 'I don't want to be picking you up with a broken skull.'

He looks down at her wide red face, eyes wrinkled against the sun, veil a bit crooked. 'It's not steep, Sister, not like the roof at home. I'm the one gets the tennis balls down. I'm used to it. Heck, you got a lot of stuff in this guttering. There's even grass growing in it.'

'Grass?' Sister Mary Clare laughs. 'Well, now, isn't nature wonderful? Imagine grass growing so far off the ground. What did you do this time, Brian?'

'Blasphemery.' He runs the garden trowel along the iron guttering and tries to scoop up the rubbish that has packed down to compost with moss and grass on top. 'Uncharitable thinking.' The trowel is useless. He thrusts his fingers into the gunk and a great gutter-shaped wad of it comes up in his hand. He holds it up so that Sister Mary Clare can see it. 'This hasn't been cleaned out for years and years.'

'That would be the truth of it,' she says. 'Can you see me up a ladder? All I can say is it's a happy fault that gets the garden weeded and the gutters cleaned. You're a good worker, Brian, for the age of you.'

He pulls out another mat of gunk knitted with grass roots, shows it to her and drops it into the bucket. 'Sister,' he says, 'can you get into heaven if you hate someone?'

She thinks about that. 'Hate is an ugly thing,' she says.

'What about hating a murderer or someone who starts a war?'

'Brian, what Himself tells us is to hate the action but to love the person who's doing it.'

He knew she was going to say that. He's heard it before. He says, 'But suppose you get it wrong. Suppose you try to love someone who's doing something really, really bad, and it doesn't work. You hate them just a little bit, and then you die. Do you go to heaven?'

She smiles. 'I wouldn't be bothering your head, Brian. Let me tell you something. When you get to heaven, first thing you see is St Peter at the gate. You look through the gate and you see Himself standing inside and behind Himself there's the Father on a big high throne. Well, you won't be worrying at all, about any of that. You'll be going all the way around to the back of heaven, right to the very back, and there you'll see Himself's mother standing by an open window. The window's always open, you know. Our Lady never refuses any soul that wants in.'

The breath comes out of him in pure relief as he pulls up more rubbish. He likes this job. It gives him the same kind of satisfaction as picking scabs and squeezing boils.

Sister Mary Clare says, 'I'm after believing you've got the vocation, Brian Collins. I think God is calling you to the priesthood.'

A part of him is pleased to hear that but he wants more. He wants to be a saint, so pure that he shines like snow and his mother, looking down from heaven, sees him bright as a star and says to the angels, 'That bright light down there! That's my Brian.' But then there is another part of him that wants to be an electrical engineer like his father and spend a summer at Scott Base fixing generators and looking at penguins in real snow. Oh, but that's not all of it. There's the third part of him that given half a chance would pee in Liz Fletcher's coffee and not be the least bit sorry to see her drink it.

* * *

When the bucket is nearly full, he lowers it to Sister Mary Clare and she takes it to the compost heap. She walks very slowly, swaying from side to side, and he thinks again about nuns having legs up to their knees. It's not true, but that's the way she moves. While she is emptying the bucket, he stands on the hip of the roof and stretches out his arms imagining what it would be like to be a seagull. He could take off across the lawn, glide down the hill to the beach and then fly over the sea, clear across to Australia or, if he were an albatross, maybe even to Antarctica where the sun stays up in the middle of summer. He's seen it in his father's photo album, a golden ball sitting on top of a snowy mountain and underneath, the word *midnight* in his father's writing.

His sister Kathy said that Mum wouldn't have got ill if their Dad hadn't spent six months away at Scott Base, but that was stupid. Cancer just happened to people for no reason. Anyway, he didn't know what Kathy was going on about because she and Beth and Nicky were all over Dad's girlfriend as though Mum had never been there. Even Joey. Although there was an excuse for Joey because he was too little to remember their mother. Kathy and Beth were the worst. Just because Liz brought them lollies and painted their fingernails red like her own, they let her shift the furniture around and use Mum's best tea things.

When Brian told Kathy he'd seen Dad and Liz kissing, Kathy laughed. 'She's got her claws into him,' she said but not in an angry way, more as though getting your claws into someone was a clever thing to do.

His teacher said that in Alaska there were eagles that caught salmon with their claws and if a salmon was too big, it could take the eagle into the water and it would drown. He asked Dad if there were eagles in Antarctica. There weren't. No salmon, either. The biggest bird was the wandering albatross and mostly it ate krill which were like shrimps.

He lifts one leg and wobbles on the roof, arms outstretched, daring to close his eyes for a moment, to imagine icebergs as big as castles beneath him. When he opens his eyes again, he sees that the bucket is coming back and Sister Mary Clare is looking up, smiling. He bends his arms to show her that he's just been stretching and walks back to the ladder.

'I was thinking you were a bird, Brian Collins,' she says, leaning against the ladder and reaching up so that her sleeves fall away showing thick arms as pink as her face. 'Like the fairy folk back home always changing into birds to build nests in the chimney in the spring. So all summer long, smoke fills your room and there's not a blind thing you can do about it without offending the little people. Come end of summer, though, when they be turning back and leaving the nest, you go up and find a gold fairy piece sitting in the straw for your troubles.'

He sets the bucket on the other side of the roof and kneels beside it. 'You ever got a gold fairy piece?' he asks.

'I heard of it,' she says.

'Can you spend fairy gold?'

'Well that's the thing now.' Her voice is smiling. 'Being a gift from the little folk, it never leaves you. You spend the gold coin in a shop and on the way home, there it is again in your pocket.'

He thinks about that and laughs with the deliciousness of it, a gold coin that keeps coming back like a boomerang. But he knows he can't allow himself to believe it. 'Nah!' he says, dumping rubbish into the bucket.

'There's plenty will tell you,' she says. 'My mother knew a few who for all their spending never ran out of money. But if you destroyed a nest in your chimney, then it was the chicken dropping you got. My mother used to say it had the terrible smell, and as fast as you threw it away it turned up back in your pocket, sticking as close as glue.'

He imagines chicken poo that can't be thrown away, sitting in Liz Fletcher's red handbag. 'It's just a story,' he says.

Sister Mary Clare comes to his side of the garage, squeezing herself between the wall and the fence. 'There's older things than St Patrick,' she says. 'Are you nearly finished?'

'No birds' nests, Sister,' he jokes. 'No chimney.'

She looks up at him, her face now serious. 'There's a batch of jam tarts in the fridge. I made them myself this morning.'

* * *

He takes his shoes off at the back door and goes into the laundry to scrub his hands. Sister Mary Clare, holding the towel for him, says there's no need to run down to the presbytery because Father Friel is coming to the convent for his tea and Brian just might like to be having absolution in the convent chapel, then he can eat with them, lasagne tonight, and Father Friel can be putting the bicycle on the back of his car and giving him a lift home to his Da's before bedtime, and what does he think of that?

'Choice,' he says.

'Go on into the kitchen,' says Sister Mary Clare. 'Tell them I say you're to have cocoa and jam tarts.'

* * *

All three of the Sisters wear glasses, although he doesn't know why Sister Luke bothers, since she is so blind that she can't read the name of the newspaper. 'Brian, is this the *Dominion* or the *Evening Post?*' she asks.

Several times he's read the newspaper to her. It's usually old news because they get their papers handed on from Father Friel, who forgets to put them in their mail box. The nuns don't have TV. Sister Agnes says television is a waste of time and money and most of the programmes are hardly what you call decent.

Sister Luke sits at the table, her wrinkled white hands folded around her rosary beads, which drop and clatter softly on the edge of the tabletop. 'Will you be a good lad and read me the goings-on in the government?'

It's not interesting news she wants, not the murders or fires and crashes, but boring stuff about Parliament, Mr Muldoon says this, Mr Rowling says that. He keeps his finger under the lines of print and struggles with words like *employment conditions* and *criminal jurisdiction* although he gets some help from Sister Agnes, who is chopping carrots on a board at the sink.

'The organ—organ—is—a—t—'

'Organisation,' says Sister Agnes.

'Organ–isation for Econ–omic Co–co–'

'Co-operation,' Sister Agnes says.

'Co-operation and de–velop–ment calls for further m–mea–s– measures to expose the local manu–fact–uring sector–'

Sister Luke puts her hand up as though she is trying to stop traffic. Her fingers wave in the air, advancing to touch his face, his arm, then down to the paper. She frowns, her thin mouth looking as though it's sewn shut with long stitches. Her eyes stare somewhere over his head. 'We had that psalm yesterday,' she says.

Brian looks at Sister Agnes, who wipes her hands on her apron.

'Yesterday's psalm,' Sister Luke insists.

Sister Agnes touches Sister Luke on the shoulder and says, 'Sister, the boy has finished. It's time for him to have his cocoa.'

'Cocoa.' Sister Luke smiles. 'That's nice. We always had cocoa in winter although I find now too much gives me a headache.' She rubs her rosary beads between the thumbs and forefingers of both hands. 'You read that psalm beautifully, Brian. Thank you.'

'That's all right,' he says.

'Would you like to read me another?' she asks.

He looks to Sister Agnes, who smiles, shakes her head at him, then says to Sister Luke, 'Do you know what Brian has done today, Luke? He's cleaned the guttering on the garage roof. It was so choked with dead leaves that the water was running down the walls.'

'Oh?' says Sister Luke. 'You got up on the ladder? What a courageous boy! You know, we're not good with ladders. God bless you, Brian. It was a very kind thing.'

'My penance for blasphemery,' he says, lest she give him too much credit.

'Call it a ladder to heaven,' says Sister Agnes, back to chopping carrots.

Both Sisters laugh, high laughter like tinkling glass, and he feels uncomfortable that they should joke about something as serious as sin. 'I haven't had absolution yet,' he says.

Sister Agnes scoops the chopped carrots into a saucepan. 'Father Friel will be here soon. I phoned your Dad and told him you were having tea with us.'

'What did he say?'

She holds the saucepan under the tap. 'That you were a lucky little tinker and you were to do the dishes.'

He laughs. 'I don't mind. I do dishes all the time at home.'

'Get along with you,' says Sister Agnes. 'I made up the dishes part.'

* * *

It is much easier to be good at the convent. At home, every space is filled with stuff, bits of toys, food, clothes, Joey's wet nappies, tools, things his father is fixing, and there is always noise with the stereo and TV, kids bawling and fighting and Dad yelling at them to shut the flaming up. It's as quiet as sunlight here and the rooms are practically empty except for a few chairs and tables, and a piano in the front room next to the bookcase, and a statue of St Joseph, missing patches of paint, inside the front door. He thinks that the furniture in the convent is like the Sisters, old, comfortable, quiet, not much for such a big space. He walks around the lounge, sitting in each chair in turn, and practises feeling good with his head full of thoughts about cleaning the guttering and having lasagne with four holy people, although he's not sure about Father Friel, who sometimes swears and kicks his car. At least it's plain swearing and not blasphemery so he probably only has to confess to himself. Lasagne with four holy people and his mother looking down on him from heaven and saying, that's my Brian.

He wants to touch everything in the room, each book, the picture of mist on a mountain, the picture of a Maori Mary holding Jesus in her cloak, the piano with its teeth just showing under the lid, the ledges under the windows. There is now a wind dancing on the sea, kicking up whiteness almost as bright as snow, and there is yellow in the sky where the sun is setting.

The thing he remembers most about his mother in hospital is the smell. He wants to forget it and remember other things like her eyes and the way she squeezed his fingers, but it is always the smell that comes back, rotten, like a sheep that's been dead for a long time. He puts his face against the window and breathes slowly.

Glass has a smell. He had this big argument at school with Bryce Pettigrew, who said glass had no smell at all, and Beth, with her blocked nose, agreed with Bryce. Trust Beth. The glass in front of him smells like cold days before rain, and the wooden frames smell like a cupboard under a sink. He sniffs the pale blue curtains. They have a kind of dry, old smell, like shoes that have been left out in the sun until they've curled.

'So there you are!' says Sister Mary Clare, coming in with a plastic shopping bag. 'In honour of your visit, we're having a special treat.' She waves the bag at him. 'Ice-cream.'

He doesn't tell her that he has ice-cream nearly every night because it's the easiest pudding Dad can think of. 'What sort?' he asks.

'Vanilla,' she says.

He nods at the rightness of the choice. The ice-cream will be white and holy like snow.

* * *

Father Friel takes him into the convent chapel and they sit in the front chairs by the Blessed Sacrament. The priest looks as though he could be Sister Mary Clare's brother, having the same height and width and the same redness of face. Brian doesn't know what Sister Mary Clare's hair is like but Father Friel's is short all the way up his pink neck and then curly grey on top. His nose is different from Sister Mary Clare's and so are his eyes, which are pale grey and bulgy, moving around so much that Brian wonders if it's possible for eyes to be double-jointed.

24

'You're a smart boy and you mean no harm,' Father Friel says.

Brian's not sure that he has understood. 'It was a blasphemery against the Holy Name, Father.'

Father Friel scratches his ear. 'Are you sure you're not overdoing it?'

He doesn't know what the priest means, so he stays silent, his hands between his knees.

'It's been hard for you since your mother died, hasn't it?'

He nods.

'And you like coming here to the good Sisters, hmm? It's not like having your mother back, but it's not hardship either. Cocoa and biscuits. Bit of attention. How old are you now, Brian?'

'Eight.'

'Are you doing all right at school?'

'Yes, Father.'

'And at home? Ah, you got all those sisters, haven't you? I know, I know, I had sisters too. Your father, well, he's got a lot on his plate, he has, trying to keep his business going and his family. How old's your little brother now? Two?'

'It was blasphemery, Father.'

'So you said. What was the sin last Tuesday?'

He wriggles and swings his feet under the chair. 'I told my sister Beth to get run over by a bus.'

'Why'd you say that?'

'She – she reckoned glass didn't have any smell.'

Father Friel lets out a long breath. 'Brian, how many times have you been sent to the convent these past three weeks?'

'I – I don't know, Father.'

'Don't know? Now there's a fine thing. If confession was at all important, you'd think you'd remember, wouldn't you?'

He doesn't answer.

Father Friel takes a pen out of his pocket and puts the blunt end in his ear. He shakes the pen a little, removes it and looks closely at it before putting it back in his pocket. 'There might be an easier way around this, Brian. You like coming here and the good Sisters appreciate your help, so why not just come and do chores two or three times a week, hmm? No excuses? That might save us all a lot of bother.'

He looks up to see the priest's eyes swivel knowingly. He looks away again and nods.

'Fair enough,' says Father Friel. 'I'll have a little word with your Dad. After this, you can say five Hail Marys for pestering God with trumped-up sins. Bow your head and be sharp about it. The tea's getting cold.'

CHAPTER THREE

THE FIRST TIME HE SLEEPS AT THE CONVENT, IT'S BECAUSE THE light on his bike doesn't work. His Dad can't come and get him on account of him being too busy installing heating in a new factory, and Liz who's baby-sitting can't leave the others in the middle of their meal or so she says. Brian knows better.

'She hates me,' he announces.

Sister Agnes shakes a long finger at him. 'That's an uncharitable thought and unworthy of you, Brian.'

He feels misunderstood. 'I didn't say I hated her. I said she hates me. She does. It's because I'm like my Mum.'

Sister Agnes gives his nose a tap that almost stings. 'Brian Collins, you're the image of your father's father, and you've still got a black spot in your thinking where that young woman is concerned. Don't you think you should say a little prayer about it?'

He doesn't answer but steps back, turning his head away from her finger. He wonders if a black spot is the start of having a hole in the brain like Sister Luke who forgets the names of things. It's this hole in my brain, she often says. The words fall right out of sight.

He doesn't want a hole in his brain. Sister Luke's is getting so big that there are times when she forgets who she is.

'You make your peace with Elizabeth tomorrow,' says Sister Agnes. 'Tonight you can stay here.'

Stay the night at the convent? He looks at the three faces and now they are all smiling, especially Sister Mary Clare, who has her shoulders scrunched up and her arms folded as though she's trying to stop herself from bursting wide open with laughter.

'Do you want to stay?' Sister Luke asks.

He nods, then remembering that she can't see, says, 'Yes, please.'

'You can have the extern's room,' says Sister Agnes.

He knows where that is. It's the only bedroom downstairs and it's at the back of the building tucked between the bathroom and the laundry, a narrow room with a high window, a bed with a pink fluffy cover and a picture of the Sacred Heart. Sister Mary Clare once told him it had been a room for girls in trouble. He thinks it will be dead right for him because he's always in trouble, especially on account of that you-know-who woman who's chasing after his father, and there are times when he feels he'll never get to be a saint.

Sister Mary Clare brings out a big plastic bag full of clothes donated by the parish, children's garments which she has washed and ironed for the St Vincent de Paul shop. 'They're a little shabby but clean,' she says, sorting through them. There are no pyjamas his size but she finds a T-shirt and track pants and Sister Agnes fills a hot-water bottle from the kettle.

They stand by his bed to say his prayers with him and then each of them touches his forehead with a blessing before putting out the light. He lies in the darkness, holding the hot-water bottle to his chest, and lets the goodness of the room overtake him. It has a faint lemon smell, this room for kids in trouble, and it is very quiet except for the distant creaking of Sister Mary Clare's footsteps on the stairs. He can feel the room's goodness working on him like warm milk and now he doesn't even want to think of that stupid Liz woman. Instead, he imagines his mother, shining like a star in the sky above the convent, and him, very sleepy, shining back.

As winter comes on and the days get shorter, he spends more nights at the convent. He bikes up the hill after school to fetch the Sisters' firewood from the garage and stack it by the back door. Then he goes in for cocoa and biscuits. Sometimes he reads to Sister Luke and sometimes he's sent down to the shops by Sister Mary Clare. He does his homework on the kitchen table with Sister Agnes, who was once a schoolteacher, hearing his spelling.

His father said that Sister Agnes used to be a real Tartar in the old days and if the kids in her class played up she'd wallop them with a ruler until they bawled. Brian thinks this might be one of his father's stories. Sister Agnes never hits him but she does tap with her finger, on the table, on his arm and, occasionally, on his nose.

'Saints preserve us, Brian Collins! I've seen better writing done by a fly crawling out of a milk jug!'

On a wet afternoon, when Sister Luke is having one of her hole-in-the-brain spells, Sister Mary Clare asks him to polish the long linoleum hall upstairs. The polish is made in a dented saucepan by Sister Agnes, beeswax and kerosine and stuff, and he wipes it, still warm from the stove, onto the green lino with a bit of rag. The convent looks different upstairs, just a long hallway with varnished boards on either side of linoleum, and a row of closed doors with holy water stoops outside. He counts the doors, sixteen, then when Sister Mary Clare goes downstairs to get polishing cloths, he opens each one a little way, to look inside. Two toilets, a bath and a shower, a hall cupboard and twelve bedrooms. The bedrooms are disappointing, a bed with a mat beside it, a dressing table and a wardrobe, nothing to say which rooms are used by the Sisters, except for some medicine on one of the dressing tables. In the bedroom at the end of the corridor, the roof is leaking, water ping-pinging into an enamel bowl on the floor.

He hears Sister Mary Clare's heavy tread and goes back to spreading the polish. When she comes near, he asks, 'What are all these rooms for?'

She is puffing from the climb. 'God bless you, Brian – a busy place it was – in the old days with eleven of us – and three lay Sisters to lend a hand and all – all sorts of work going on.'

'What did you do, Sister Mary Clare?'

'Faith and sure, what didn't we do?' She leans against the wall, folding her arms against a bunch of rags. 'It was all for families, you understand, helping the mothers and the children, especially when the menfolk were out of work or sick. I was after running a nursery down the church hall for the little ones while their mothers went shopping or to doctor's appointments, but it was Sister Luke who had the true charisma of St Joseph the Labourer, though to look at her now you'd not be believing she was as strong as a cart donkey. All that lawn outside? Sister Luke was after digging that into potatoes for needy families and, well, she and Sister Agnes would be hoeing till evening prayers most nights of the week, or bagging the taties for delivery. During the day, well, it was teaching for Sister Agnes, and Sister Magdalena, too. The school was all staffed by nuns in those days.' She opens her arms and drops the rags on the floor. 'God between us and all harm, Brian, we're the last of the dinosaurs, just the three of us. No Sisters in Australia now, and the mother house in Ireland has gone.'

He looks up at her. 'None of you in the whole world?'

She shakes her head. 'We were never after being a big congregation and then with the changes and no new vocations. But not to be worrying, Brian. Isn't it God's work after all, and won't he always be sending people to do it? Like you coming along on a day when my back is too bad for the polishing.'

'You should get an electric polisher,' he says.

'And us believing in the goodness of hard work?' she says with a laugh.

'Why?'

'Sure, and a simple job well done is food for the soul, Brian. Work with reverence, we say. When you've finished that lot, your own soul'll be shining like a lovely mirror.'

Maybe, but in that long hallway on his hands and knees, it's going to take him all afternoon to rub the polish to a shine and he thinks that if he had an electric polisher, his soul wouldn't feel too cheated. He sighs and Sister Mary Clare, who always seems to know what he's thinking, tells him there is an easier way. She kicks off her black slippers, sets them on the top stair, then places each of her wide woolly feet on a polishing rag. She slides along in a gliding walk, one hand on the wall for balance.

He jumps up and grabs a clean rag for each foot. He wraps them around his socks, then he's off down the corridor with sliding steps. This is easier. It's also fun. He goes faster, faster, no wall for support, and soon he can run and slide all the way to the end wall.

Sister Mary Clare claps. 'You're a good skater, Brian Collins.'

He laughs. 'I've never been on skates.' It's almost true. His sister Kathy got skates last Christmas but when he tried to borrow them, she pushed him over. He curls his toes in their grey socks to get a better grip of the polishing rags and takes another run, arms outstretched. 'This would be a neat place for skates, Sister,' he says.

'Chance would be a fine thing,' she replies. 'Roller-skates on our polished floor? If I were you I wouldn't be mentioning that to Sister Agnes.'

It doesn't matter, he tells himself. He will skate the convent way on a pair of polishing rags and the floor will shine like glass and so will his soul.

* * *

The pipes for the upstairs plumbing run down his bedroom wall and it is the gurgling and rattling that is his call to prayer in the mornings. He doesn't have to go to prayer, says Sister Agnes, but he wants to be with them in the chapel with the heaters going, and the candle flickering and the air smelling of incense. They always look as though they've been up for hours, their faces glowing and the candlelight shining on their glasses and silver crucifixes, as they recite their prayers. Sister Luke can't read the book but that doesn't matter because she knows the words off by heart.

Lord, open our lips,
and we shall praise your name.

Come, ring out our joy to the Lord;
hail the God who saves us.
Let us come before him, giving thanks,
with songs let us hail the Lord.

They give Brian a book but he's too slow and keeps losing his place. The prayers are mostly psalms and not very interesting but he likes the bits where they sing in thin high voices and he tries to join in. He knows that people have to learn these things if they're going to be saints.

I call with all my heart; Lord hear me,
I will keep your commands.
I call upon you, save me
and I will do your will.

My eyes watch for you before dawn.

I rise before dawn and cry for help,
I hope in your word.
I call upon you, save me
and I will do your will.

My eyes watch for you before dawn.

At the time of intercessory prayer, the Sisters remember everyone in the parish who is sick or burdened. He wants to pray about his trouble with that woman Liz who is now practically living in his mother's house but he is worried that if he starts telling God about it, his mother will hear. How will she feel, dead just over a year and already being replaced by someone with red fingernails? He wishes he could stop worrying about it. The goodness of the room for people in trouble only works while he is in it and as soon as he's back home, the anger returns with lightning and thunderclaps.

* * *

His biggest disappointment is the lack of support from his mother's family. Nanna Grayson, Uncle Eric and Aunty Molly, Aunty Deb, cousin Bede, they all tell him what a good thing it is that his father has found someone to help out.

'I'm sure your mother had a hand in that,' says Uncle Eric, trying to light his pipe.

Brian scowls. He knows why they have come to visit. Dad's put them up to it. Have a word to Brian, his Dad has said. The kid's being bloody difficult.

'She's a nice young woman,' says Nanna. 'Not beautiful like your mother, but no one'll ever replace your mother. You've got to admit Elizabeth's heart's in its right place.'

'You won't find many women who'll take on five children,' says Aunty Deb.

'She's not!' Brian cries.

They look at each other and Uncle Eric burns his fingers on his match.

'She's not taking us on!' he yells, and he runs out of the house.

Beth and Nicky are playing hopscotch on the path outside the kitchen windows, Nicky balancing one-legged like a flamingo, and already fluttering with alarm. 'Go away, Brian! Leave us alone or I'll tell on you. Brian?'

He pushes her and she falls, squawking her head off, while Beth rushes for the house, yelling, 'Brian hit Nicky! He hit her and she didn't do anything to him!'

Nicky makes the most of it. She lies across hopscotch squares, screaming as though he's broken all her arms and legs. Nanna Grayson comes out the back door, Aunty Molly and Aunty Deb close behind.

33

He runs around the house and hides in the garden shed, behind some sacks and bales of pea straw, until they've forgotten him.

* * *

The next time he goes to the convent he finds that the fluffy pink bedspread has gone, replaced by a blanket that has a picture of Elvis playing a guitar.

'We thought you'd like something more modern,' says Sister Agnes. 'More with it, as you young people say. It didn't cost anything. We did an outright exchange at the St Vincent de Paul shop.'

He doesn't think that Elvis Presley is all that modern but he is pleased that the fluffy pink cover has gone.

'Tell me what it looks like,' says Sister Luke.

'It's light brown,' he says, 'and Elvis is dark brown and white. He's got a microphone. He's playing his guitar and singing.'

'What's he singing?' she asks.

He looks at her, then says, 'I don't know, Sister.'

'I thought it might have the words on it.'

'No, Sister. Just a picture of Elvis.'

Sister Luke laughs. 'Isn't that a funny thing. Elvis is an anagram of evils.'

He frowns. 'What's an anagram?'

'It'll be just as warm as the pink bedspread,' says Sister Mary Clare.

'Two words with the same letters,' says Sister Luke. 'Elvis. Evils.'

'Elvis is just Elvis,' says Sister Agnes in a schoolteacher voice.

'And Brian is an anagram of brain,' Sister Luke adds, her eyes like frosted windows behind her glasses.

Elvis, evils, he thinks, evils on the Brian, on the brain. Liz Fletcher of the stoves and dishwashing machines at Bidwell's Home Appliances is all the evils in his life in one person and he can't stop hating her.

That evening he pulls off the blanket and stuffs it in the

wardrobe. He wakes several times in the night, his feet and shoulders aching with cold, and comforts himself with the half-formed thought that this is what goodness is like, a continent of snow and ice and he, Brian Collins, is lying in the middle of it with frost in his hair and the white light of heaven all around him.

* * *

Once a month there is a school Mass and they walk in a long line from the school to the church, passing the convent which stands tall on its hill, smoke curling from the back chimney.

It pleases Brian to think that the fire is going because he looks after the Sisters, stacking loads of dry pine wood at the door, and cleaning the ash from their grate.

Matthew Cuttance also turns his head to the old building and says, 'It looks like a haunted house. Looks like a loony bin.'

Brian wants to punch stupid Cuttance on his stupid skinny face but he can't because he's going to Mass, and Cuttance knows it.

'Brian Collins is going to be a nun,' jeers Matthew, who is a heathen and doesn't care what he says.

All the kids know that Brian sometimes stays at the convent and those who have got over feeling sorry for him because of his mother are giving him a hard time. Brian gives Matthew a cold look. 'You'll keep,' he says.

'What colour are their knickers?' Matthew jumps up and down. 'You ever see their knickers on the line?'

'Shut up, Cuttance,' says Bryce Pettigrew, for once on Brian's side.

'Nuns' knickers, nuns' knickers,' chants Matthew.

'Shut up!' Brian yells.

Mr Siataga calls down the line, 'Enough from you, Collins! See me in my office after Mass.'

'Nuns' knickers!' whispers Matthew, grinning all over his stupid face.

His mother always came to the school Masses. He remembers how she used to blow him a kiss off the top of her fingers as he walked past and how embarrassed and pleased he'd felt. The Sisters never turn their heads as he goes down to the front pews. From the back they look like three dark grey towers, the folds in their veils as still as concrete. As he walks past, he looks back and sees three sets of glasses over closed eyes, lips moving without a sound. He wants them to look at him, give some special sign that he belongs, but they don't even glance his way, although they usually speak to him after Mass. But that doesn't count because they talk to everyone after Mass. Some mornings he can only see the top of Sister Agnes's veil, there are so many people standing around. The Sisters must know every single person in St Mary's parish.

His father reckons it's a thundering great pity the lazy sods in the parish don't get up the hill and give the good Sisters a helping hand, but that's usually when his Dad's late for work because he's been putting a new element in the convent hot-water cylinder or fixing the lights where rain has got in on the wiring.

John and Gregory, the Molloy brothers, are altar servers today. Another year and Brian will be old enough to be up there with all that holiness in his hands. He will light the candles with great care, hold the missal, and pass the censer to Father Friel, letting the fragrant smoke go up to heaven where his mother sits with the Mother of God, talking about their sons.

Mum always told him that one day he'd be an altar boy.

Father Friel is late. He comes in wearing a green sweatshirt with I DRIVE A FERRARI across it, which is not true because he drives a 1972 Ford, and a piece of white paper with blood on it stuck on his chin. He looks at the kids clattering into the pews, says something to the Molloy boys and rushes back to the sacristy.

'Move further down, Brian,' says Mrs Neal, the infant teacher.

He has to slide all the way to the end of the seat next to Matthew Cuttance, who grins and says in a loud whisper, 'Collins is going to be a nun.'

He pretends not to hear. He goes down on the kneeler, blesses himself and closes his eyes.

'Sister Brian wears nuns' knickers, yeh, yeh, yeh!'

That does it. He punches Matthew Cuttance fair in the gob.

* * *

'What in the blazes did you think you were doing?' says his father, who has come home from work to have Kathy fill his ears with the story.

He can't tell him.

'If anybody wants my opinion,' says Beth, shaking pepper over the mashed potatoes, 'Matthew Cuttance has been asking for that for the longest time.' She gives Brian an admiring look. 'You should have seen the blood. They got a bucket and a mop.'

'Excuse me,' says Kathy. 'Excuse me, please, we just so happen to be talking about a church.'

'Are you going to tell me or aren't you?' His father hits the table with his fist, jiggling the knives and forks.

He shrugs, tired of questions, and keeps his head down.

'You realise,' says his father, 'that if you were older you could have been arrested for assault.'

Kathy says, 'G.B.H. It means grievous bodily harm.'

He knows what it means.

'Matthew Cuttance bawled and bawled.' Nicky, enjoying the drama, straightens her cutlery. 'Brian had to go to see Mr Siataga.'

'I've tried, so help me!' roars his father. 'I've bent over backwards to make allowances for you. Do you think you're the only one in this family missing your mother? Do you now?'

He wants to say that his mother has nothing to do with it, but it is too much of an effort to reach the words. Tomorrow will be worse. He won't be able to go to the convent because Sister Agnes will wag her finger in his face and demand to know why he punched a classmate in church. He looks at the knuckles of his right hand which are swollen red with patches of blue.

He is a martyr.

* * *

Father Friel comes to the door of the presbytery with a slice of toast halfway to his mouth. 'Ah,' he says. 'I was expecting you.'

'I couldn't come yesterday,' he explains. 'Mr Siataga kept me in after school and then I had to –'

'You'd better come in,' says Father Friel.

He is expecting to go to the back of the church and the confessional but instead he is led into the presbytery and told to sit down at the kitchen table half-covered with a newspaper.

'Had your breakfast?'

'Yes, Father.'

'Want some toast?'

'No, thank you, Father. Father, I've come to see you –'

'I know why you've come,' says the priest. He sits down and his eyes swivel over the paper which is open at the sports page.

Brian takes a deep breath. 'Father, are saints prosecuted?'

'What?'

'Saints. Do they get prosecuted?'

Father Friel looks at him. He picks up his teacup and sucks it with a noise like a straw at the bottom of a milkshake. 'I think you mean persecuted.'

'Yes. Yes, that's it.'

'How did it start?' Father Friel nods at his bruised hand.

He puts his arm down at his side. 'Can I – can I have confession and not say why?'

'The Cuttance boy, did he say something about your mother?'

'No.'

'Your father and his friend?'

He shakes his head.

Father Friel leans across the table and his eyes flicker over Brian's face. 'Was it about the convent?' he says.

Brian nods.

'So now, what did he say that you made him bleed like a stuck pig? Not to mention the unholy riot at Mass. Hmm?'

The thick words in Brian's throat dissolve and he starts to cry, quietly at first and then with sobs like loud hiccups.

Father Friel has another drink of tea. 'Take your time,' he says.

So he blurts out what he can't tell his Dad or Mr Siataga, and Father Friel listens although he pretends to read the sports pages. When it's over Brian explains between sobs that he can never go back to the convent again because the Sisters will want to know Matthew's words.

Father Friel turns over a page of the paper but he nods to show he understands. 'How would it be if I smoothed things over for you? I'll be seeing the good Sisters after Mass this morning.'

'You won't tell them!'

'I won't say a word that'll be getting you in trouble or embarrassment of any kind. Trust me?' He smiles and his bulgy eyes are friendly. 'Trust me?' he says again.

Brian nods. 'Yes, Father.'

'You'd better run along to school.'

'What about confession, Father?'

'Ah. Well. I think that can wait until your hand is healed. Are you playing rugby this year?'

'Soccer, Father.'

'Saturday matches?'

'Yes, Father.'

'That won't do any harm at all. And you say you're keeping up with your school work?'

'Yes, Father.'

'Well, if I were you I wouldn't be worrying too much about the state of your soul, not unless you want to be telling God he didn't know what he was doing when he made you.'

'No, Father, I don't want to do that.'

'Don't worry so much about things, Brian. Let time do its healing. Well, off you go. You know the way out.'

He leaves Father Friel's kitchen table, feeling no better, the bruised hand hardly painful compared with the weight of a sin that the priest had treated like a feather. Mum is a saint in heaven. Everybody says so. If he doesn't get to be a saint too, how will he ever see her again?

What if he dies now? What if? Excuse me, God, he wants to say in a Kathy voice, excuse me, but I really don't think you knew what you were doing when you made Brian Collins.

* * *

Father Friel is right about one thing, though. He does fix things up with the Sisters. That afternoon Brian goes up to the convent with shaky stomach and legs, but they don't mention the fight in church, not one word, and when he has finished stacking the firewood by the back door, they give him a slice of lemon meringue pie.

CHAPTER FOUR

H IS FATHER SAYS THEY ARE HAVING THE PARTY BECAUSE
Nicky's seventh birthday falls on a Saturday, but anyone
can see it's not Nicky's party. The house is full of adults,
including Nanna, Aunty Deb, people from Dad's work and Mr
Bidwell who owns Bidwell's Home Appliances, where Liz Fletcher
sells stoves with ovens that clean themselves. Nicky has a couple of
friends from school and a birthday cake, but the table and bench in
the kitchen are covered with beer bottles and the air is layered with
banners of cigarette smoke which wave when someone opens the
back door.

It wasn't breezy this morning. The wind came up about eleven
as people started arriving and it has been blowing flat out ever since.
His mother's cherry blossom tree is practically wrecked. The pink
flowers are being tossed about as though Mum is actually inside the
tree, shaking the branches.

It is not Nicky's party at all. It's all about Dad and Liz showing
off to their friends.

Liz no longer pretends to like Brian. The smile she has for the
girls and Joey disappears when he walks into the room and she gives

him a careful look, which is all right with him, just fine. He's given up saying the things that have to go to confession and now he doesn't talk to her at all. He pretends she's not there, and if she has cooked a meal for them, he's not hungry.

His parents' wedding photo still hangs in the sitting room but these days no one talks about Joe and Paula. It's all Joe and Liz. Even Nanna, all smiling with her hair newly permed and a blue brooch in her lace blouse, is Liz this and Liz that, in the kitchen helping to put sandwiches on the best tea-set plates and talking about a discount on a toasted sandwich maker.

Brian goes to his bedroom, lies on the bed and tries to read a comic. Fat chance. His father comes in, yanks him off by the back of his T-shirt and says if he doesn't get out there and be civilised pronto, he's not going to the convent all next week.

This is the latest. A few months ago he was being sent to the convent for punishment. Now he's kept away for the same reason.

He goes to the bathroom, thinking no one can interrupt him there, but he's wrong because they've all been drinking loads of beer. 'Coming, coming!' he calls. He sees a lipstick by the washbasin. He doesn't know whose it is but he grabs it, twists off the top and writes the figure 14 on the mirror. 'All right! I'm coming!'

Fourteen. It's the number of months since his mother died. He hopes they all see it, especially Dad, and that they remember and feel absolutely rotten.

* * *

Nearly everyone has gone by five o'clock. His father is in the sitting room with Joey asleep against him, and the girls are helping to clean up the kitchen. Brian puts the empty DB bottles in the crates outside, then cleans the lipstick off the bathroom mirror because he doesn't want Liz to do it. He sits in his mother's armchair, opposite his father, and looks at the wedding photo on the wall, his Dad young as a high school boy and his mother smiling like the winner of a beauty contest. He's sure she's smiling for him, although he wasn't even in her thoughts when the photo was taken, and he knows she's pleased that he's faithful to her memory. But there is a problem, small and deeply secret, to add to his list of troubles. He's forgetting what his mother looked like. True. The images he remembers are from the hospital when she couldn't talk or breathe by herself. They're not from home in the days when she could laugh and tell stories and dance with Dad to Abba records. Sometimes small bits come to him, the feeling of her eyelashes on his cheek in a butterfly kiss, the way her voice changed pitch when she was surprised, the tooth that sometimes stuck out over her lower lip and her smile, oh yes, her smile. But these bits hardly ever come together in a complete picture. It seems that his mother is becoming someone who lives in photographs.

Joey stirs against Dad's chest and puts his thumb in his mouth.

Brian thinks that with his father half drunk and imprisoned in the chair, this would be a good time to get him to talk about Antarctica.

'Tell me about the snow?' he asks.

Dad smiles across Joey's sticky-up hair. 'Did I tell you about the Emperor penguin? The father carries the egg.'

He has said that before, but Brian still looks interested.

'There's not a scrap of anything for a nest,' Dad says. 'If the egg got laid in the snow, it'd be frozen solid in minutes. So the female lays it directly on the male penguin's feet.' He stretches out his legs and wriggles his toes over the edge of his roman sandals. 'He's got this brood slit in his feathers and he crouches over it to keep it warm.'

'Can he walk?' Brian asks.

'Sure he can walk.' Dad grins. 'It's running that's difficult.'

Brian grins.

'Well, what do you know, the sun's come out!' says Dad.

Brian looks to the window, and too late realises that his father is referring to his smile. He stands to make out that he's watching

43

something on the road, then he yawns, sits down again and says, 'I want you to tell me about the snow.'

His Dad shrugs with his eyebrows. 'Ask me something easy.'

'What's not easy?'

'Not enough words,' says Dad. 'Can you think of a thousand words for a thousand different shapes and shades of whiteness? God help me, I can't even think of a single word to describe something that's bigger than biggest. Can you?'

He shakes his head.

'Trouble is, up here you always see Antarctica in a cosy little frame. Television, magazines, movies, photographs. You get there and find yourself in something that goes on for ever. No end to it. And it's colder than hell.'

'Hell is hot,' he says.

'Don't you believe it,' says Dad. 'But I'll tell you this much, it's heaven too. You lose yourself. All that whiteness, it wraps itself around your head and sucks it out like a little grape. You forget who you are.'

Brian is not sure that he understands about the grape bit but his desire to go to Antarctica grows stronger with talk of snow. 'Are there many Catholics down there?'

'What do you mean?'

'Do they have churches and – and priests?'

'God's truth, Brian!' His father laughs. 'Don't you let those holy nuns be filling your head with vocation stuff. You're too young for that.'

'They don't,' he protests.

'Not half, they don't,' says Dad. 'There's more room in Antarctica for scientists, if you want to know – and electricians. You've got plenty of time to decide.' He shifts Joey and looks at a wet patch on his T-shirt. 'Be a good lad and ask Liz for a dry nappy.'

* * *

44

By now he has learned that much of his good feeling about the convent comes from its routine, the same activities at the same time each day. At school, he looks at the wall clock and knows exactly what is happening. 9.45 am: the Sisters are walking home from Mass. 10.30 am: Sister Mary Clare will be getting the clothes for the St Vincent de Paul shop out of the drier and Sister Luke will be folding them. Midday: Chapel and lunchtime prayer. 12.30 pm: a bowl of soup, a thick slice of bread without butter, a cup of tea and don't forget Sister Luke's heart pills. 2.00 pm: Sister Luke is having her nap while Sister Mary Clare and Sister Agnes do the mending. 2.30 pm: Sister Mary Clare delivers scones or pikelets to the drop-in centre and sometimes shops on the way home. Sister Agnes makes her phone calls. 3.00 pm: they wait for Brian.

* * *

On Mondays, Wednesdays and Fridays, he rides his bike up the hill to continue his day in their rhythm. 3.30 pm: Brian Collins stacks firewood by the back door. 4.00 pm: Brian Collins has cocoa and reads to Sister Luke. 4.30 pm: Brian does his homework. 5.30 pm: evening meal. 6.30 pm: evening prayer. When he stays the night he joins them for their hour of recreation, which usually means sewing or knitting for Sister Agnes and Sister Mary Clare, and fixing things for him. He loves to fix things. Sister Mary Clare says he's the best eight-year-old fixer-upper in the country. So far he has sharpened all the knives, put the sink plug back on its chain, taped the loose pages of the Edmonds cooking book, put new batteries in the radio, glued the handle of a cup and brought the ladder inside to change the light bulbs. No one else can get up the ladder. 8.20 pm: they put the kettle on for his hot-water bottle while he brushes his teeth. 8.30 pm: the Sisters come to his room to tuck him in, say his prayers, lean over to bless him, the scratchy cloth of their habits brushing his face, goodnight, goodnight, God keep you in his care.

His father remarks, 'I suppose they still have fish on a Friday night.'

'No,' he says.

'No? Real pre-Vatican II nuns and they've made the great leap across the centuries to meat?'

'They don't have meat, either. Fridays we eat bread and toasted cheese.'

'Bread and cheese,' his father says slowly.

'Toasted.'

'Yes, yes, mustn't forget toasted.'

'Sister Agnes says fish is too dear.'

His father nods.

The next Friday and all the Fridays after, he gives Brian five dollars to buy fish and chips for the nuns' tea at the convent.

'What a shameful waste of money,' Sister Agnes says.

* * *

Talk at the convent fits into the same kind of routine. He learns without being told that Sister Agnes and Sister Luke speak only when they have to, outside of the recreation time. Most of their work is done in silence. Sister Mary Clare too, but when she's in the garden with Brian, she talks flat out, stories about the farm in Ireland, about fairies and ogres and ancient kings, about cousins and going to town in a cart pulled by her father's bicycle instead of a pony.

'Sure and when they tied down the cider corks they'd be after leaving a bottle out untied so in the night you'd hear a fine loud pop and then you'd hear happy little feet dancing like hailstones on the roof above your bed.'

He pulls weeds from around the wrinkled stem of a rose bush and laughs at the idea of fairies dancing on a house. 'You tell neat stories, Sister Mary Clare.'

'So just a story, is it?' She scrubs his head with her hand.

'My mother told stories too,' he says. 'But they were book stories, you know, Aladdin and Pinocchio. Not funny, like yours.'

'So I'm funny, as well.' She pretends to be hurt.

'You know what I mean,' he says.

* * *

At night during recreation time, the Sisters talk about the old days when there were eleven of them living in the convent, and all as busy as bees.

'Patricia was the one,' says Sister Luke, and the others laugh.

'Who was Patricia?' he asks.

'Sister Patricia,' says Sister Agnes.

'Oh, she was by far too glamorous for the veil,' says Sister Mary Clare. 'She was for Hollywood that one, with eyelashes like carpetsweepers and lips so red in themselves they were after being an occasion of sin for half the menfolk in the parish.'

'She was very glamorous,' agrees Sister Agnes. 'It was not a vanity in her so much as the way she was made. Beauty and a love for beauty. That was Patricia. The pre-Raphaelite painters would have cherished her.'

'She looked like Mary Pickford,' says Sister Luke.

'Mary who?' he asks.

'A film star long before your day,' Sister Luke says. 'Patricia wanted to serve God but the convent wasn't her place. She was too, too –'

'Individualistic,' says Sister Agnes.

'Enthusiastic,' says Sister Luke. 'One minute she'd be walking the way she was taught in the novitiate and next second she'd see or hear something that'd have her dancing like a butterfly.'

'It drove Mother Therese mad,' says Sister Mary Clare, and they all laugh again.

'Mother Therese passed on back home in Ireland.' Sister Agnes turns her face towards Brian. 'They've all gone to heaven now.'

'Not Patricia,' Sister Mary Clare tells Brian. 'She left.'

'Left?' he asks.

'She married a man from the South Island and had three children,' says Sister Agnes. 'We still get a card from them every Christmas.'

He understands. 'Left like in *The Sound of Music*,' he says.

'No,' says Sister Mary Clare. 'Patricia was tone deaf.'

* * *

At school Matthew Cuttance and his cronies still have a go at him about staying at the convent but not out loud or in class. Brian thinks that Father Friel must have said something to the teachers, and everyone knows that Father Friel doesn't take any nonsense. Before Father Friel went into the seminary he was a boxer, which was how he got an ear like a lumpy potato. That must have been ages ago. Now the rest of him is as lumpy as his ear but his voice is still strong and he's fast on his feet. He's been known to give a lazy altar boy a swipe across the head quicker than a snake strike. So no one at school bothers Brian too much. Matthew Cuttance still calls him Sister Brian Nuns-Knickers, but only in a whisper and at a distance. Brian pretends not to hear. He does keep an eye on the convent washing-line but all he sees hanging there are sheets and pillowcases and tea towels and the clothes that get laundered for the St Vincent de Paul shop. He wonders when and where the Sisters launder their underwear. It is the one part of their routine which he doesn't know, and can't find out.

* * *

Late spring, the lawns grow so fast that he has to cut them twice a week. He likes this job, walking up and down along the top of the hill, making green stripes that look like wallpaper. The mower is old, a noisy, trembling monster which sends out a roar of grass clippings and smoke all mixed together, and the first time he used it, he saw it as some kind of dragon determined to do battle with him. He cried with frustration when it wouldn't start and then the only way he could stop it was to remove the lead from the spark plug. The Sisters couldn't help him. They'd always used hand-mowers. It was his father who left work and came up in his red van to show him how to tame the dragon and make it friendly.

So yes, he likes the old mower and is pleased when Sister Mary Clare says what a marvel he is with machinery and what would they do without him, but then in the middle of the growing season, the dragon gets ill in a way that is beyond simple cures. Two of the brackets that hold the engine to the housing break clean off and the mower collapses against the ground, dying in a shower of dirt. The hand-mower must come out of the garage.

Dad takes the dragon away, promising to weld the brackets, but until he can get around to it, all of Brian's spare time is spent pushing a hand-mower that whirls like a slow egg-beater. It's just as well the weather's too warm for fires because he doesn't have time to stack firewood. Most afternoons he misses out on his cocoa as well, and he can't read the newspaper to Sister Luke. The trouble with hand-mowing is that he has to cut the same grass at least twice, pushing the mower forward and then pulling it back, pushing it again. His arms are sore for days and then they get as hard as tree branches. He guides Sister Luke's hand to feel his biceps. 'I'm Mr Universe,' he says.

'You are Mr Boastful,' she replies. 'Go and finish the lawn.'

He thinks a prayer might stop the grass from growing so quickly and he wonders who is the patron saint of lawns. There is a book of saints in the front room but it is very old with thick pages and words so long that by the time you get to the end of them, you have forgotten the beginning. It occurs to him that since his mother is a saint, she might be the one to ask. What should he call her? Saint Paula or Saint Mum? In the end he thinks that just plain Mum will work and it does. She doesn't do a miracle on the grass but on Dad, who mends the dragon and brings it around that same afternoon. That's not all that happens. Sister Mary Clare comes back from the drop-in centre with a heavy shopping bag.

'Faith, and you'll not be believing this, Brian, but Mrs Diaz at the St Vincent de Paul shop, you know what she had? Someone brought in a sack of clothes with these in it.' She opens the bag.

They are roller-skates, the old-fashioned kind that clamp on shoes with a key to tighten them.

'I said to Mrs Diaz, now I know someone who's a natural-born skater and he's never been after having skates of his own.'

He holds the skates, one in each hand, a little camera in his mind racing over the convent, the lawn, gardens, gravel path, kitchen, his little bedroom, bathroom, carpeted lounge, chapel, music room. There is only one place. The upstairs hallway.

Sister Mary Clare, her round face pinker than ever, looks up at Sister Agnes, who has only the smallest smile. 'All right, Brian. Since it is you who does the polishing –'

All three come up the stairs and stand by while he puts on the skates. Sister Mary Clare and Sister Agnes help him to his feet.

'I'm all right,' he says, lining himself up with the straightness of the corridor. 'I can manage.'

He has done this dozens of times with polishing rags. He knows he can do it with skates. His arms spread wide like a gull, like an albatross, and he pushes forward to capture the corridor in one huge glorious swoop. But the wheels betray him. They collide, lock together, and he goes down in a fearful clatter, his feet in the air.

'Oh dear!' says Sister Luke.

Sister Mary Clare and Sister Agnes are with him, lifting, lifting, Sister Mary Clare making soothing noises and Sister Agnes saying, 'You should know, Brian, that pride goes before a fall.'

* * *

That night during prayer in the chapel, he breathes a silent thank-you to his mother for the miracles received. He wonders, is she the patron saint of lawnmowers? Or roller-skates? Perhaps there is some connection between the two. For instance, she could be the saint of things with wheels that let people down. Something like that.

Later, when the convent is in silent darkness, and he is still wide awake and thinking about her, he knows the answer. Why didn't he think of it before? It's not wheels or anything like that. His mother is the patron saint of Brian Collins.

* * *

He thinks of his mother constantly on All Saints' Day and All Souls' Day and then it is time to buy the fireworks. No one in the family celebrates Guy Fawkes' Day although Dad has watched Parliament on TV and said, 'Guy Fawkes, oh Guy Fawkes, where are you now we need you?' But they always buy fireworks to put away for New Year's Eve and usually the whole family chooses them. This year, the shopping is done on a Saturday morning and although everyone else wants to go, that is, everyone except Kathy who's got softball practice, Dad takes only Brian.

They park the van outside Woolworths and Dad waits while Brian looks at each rocket, Golden Rain, Vesuvius, Jumping Jack, Catherine Wheel and of course, crackers, red and green, big and little, like miniature sticks of dynamite. He loves their smell and when he was little, he'd sleep with a burned-out rocket under his pillow so he could dream fireworks. Now he tries to think of the others, Flower Pots for Joey, Screamers for Nicky, Rainbow Rockets for Kathy and Beth.

'Wouldn't it be better to buy a couple of five-dollar bags?' his father suggests.

'We won't get what we want,' he explains.

'Okay, okay, but I am in a bit of a hurry,' says his father.

There is no hurry once they are out of the shop. Instead of going home, Dad drives to the new ceramics factory to show Brian the ducts he's designed for heating and air-conditioning, and then later, in the factory car-park, he wants to talk about the Holy Sisters.

'They think the world of you, Brian.'

'I like them too,' he says.

'I guess when you get old like that, the little things you've always taken for granted become big. Like taking the lid off a jar or cleaning floors or walking to town to post a letter. They say they don't know what they'd do without you.'

He nods, unsure where this is leading.

'You really like it there?'

He nods again.

'Those nuns used to be very strict, you know. You're only there, well, because it's the way things have happened, and because they're on their own now, no one to tell them otherwise. Obviously, you won't have a room there for ever.'

'I know that.'

Dad winds down the window to let in some air. 'This coming and going between home and the convent has us all in a bit of a spin. How would you like to stay there full-time for the next two or three months?'

He looks at his father to see if he means it but his father is watching some ducks that are waddling past the van.

'Why?' he asks.

'I've talked to Sister Agnes about it and she's happy. I'll pay them for your keep. They could do with the extra cash.'

'Is it about Liz?'

Dad puts both hands on the steering wheel and takes a breath. 'Brian, Liz and I are getting married in two weeks' time.'

Married. The car fills up with a silence that presses against his ears until his head is full of noise. It's like waves crashing inside his ears. He feels hot. His throat hurts.

'Brian?'

'You can't!'

'I'm not asking your permission, understand? I'm telling you.

The last two years have been hard for everyone, not just you. With Liz helping out, it's starting to come right. She's a good sort. You know, Brian, your mother made me promise I'd marry again. She knew I couldn't manage –'

'She didn't! She didn't mean it. You can't marry that – that –' He bangs his head on the back of the seat. 'She's not our Mum!'

'I've talked this over with Sister Agnes –'

'I won't go to the wedding!' he yells. 'I'll never come home again.'

'A couple of months'll be a good settling period. You need some time out and Liz can do with a break from all your carrying-on.'

'She hates me!'

'She doesn't hate you at all. She's just fed up to the gills with the way you behave, and frankly, Brian, so am I. We all know how you feel about your mother, and believe me, Liz isn't trying to replace her.'

'Yes, she is!'

'You heard what I said. This isn't up for negotiation. We're being married the Saturday after next, no fuss, no honeymoon. Naturally we'd like you to be civilised about it, but your attendance at the ceremony is not compulsory.' His father turns the key and the van shudders.

He bashes his head against the seat until his skull hurts. 'You killed my mother! If you hadn't gone to Antarctica, she wouldn't have got cancer. You killed her so you could marry that Liz!'

The key is turned off and the van goes still. 'In God's name, what are you talking about?'

He has gone too far to take back the words. 'She got the cancer because you weren't there!'

'Brian, that's utter rubbish and you know it. Will you stop banging the seat? I swear I don't know what to do about you. You're nearly nine and you've got a good head on your shoulders when you're not trying to knock it out of shape, but you get some queer ideas. Think sense, boy.'

His father puts his arm across his shoulders and tries to pull him across the seat, but he jerks away, and starts crying. 'Mum is in heaven watching you!'

His father sighs. 'That's enough. You've got a fine old imagination, Brian, only you've got to learn to keep it under control. I mean it. You give your imagination permission to run wild, and you're in deep trouble. It'll take over your life and you'll end up not knowing what's true and what isn't true. I've seen people like that.'

He is crying too hard to answer.

'The most important part of any talent is the way you manage it. Remember that, Brian. I'm not worried about your feelings for your Mum, or what you think about Liz. That's natural. It's your imaginings that worry me. Keeping the faith is one thing, but this way-out religious stuff, it's not normal in a kid your age.'

'You – you can't – marry her.'

'I know the Sisters encourage it. They think you've got a vocation, and that might well be. I'm just saying, don't let it run away with you. Do you know what I'm talking about?'

He looks up and sees the factory and the car-park swimming in a goldfish bowl. He blinks and feels the itch of water running down his cheeks. 'You can't – you can't –'

'I know,' his father says, putting his hand on the back of his neck. 'You've got a storm inside you. Just give it time. We'll all give it time. It'll pass and the whole world'll look different. Do you hear, Brian? Your thinking will change, sure as eggs are eggs.'

With the hand on his neck, Brian can't shake his head but he knows that he cannot change. To accept his father marrying Liz would be to remove his mother even further from his life.

CHAPTER FIVE

S ISTER AGNES GOES TO THE WEDDING. SHE TELLS HIM IT IS A fitting tribute to his mother that his father respects the married state. 'There are many now who don't,' she says.

Because he is determined to show no interest, he has many questions he cannot ask. Dad said they were getting married in St Mary's Church with Father Friel, but were his sisters there? Nanna and Aunty Deb? Did she have a bride's dress and red fingernails and flowers in her hair? What did his father wear?

Sister Agnes looks at him over the top of her glasses. 'There wasn't a breath of wind, which is unusual for this time of year. You'd think the weather was a gift from your saintly mother. Her blessing, so to speak.' She smiles and nods, still looking at him.

He decides to pretend that the wedding wasn't real. If it's just a story that someone saw on TV and nothing to do with him, the hurting of it stops. He smiles back at Sister Agnes. 'There was a big bundle of newspapers in the letterbox, Sister. Father Friel must have put them there.'

Sister Agnes tucks her hands in her sleeves. 'Don't change the subject, Brian Collins.'

'I'm not, Sister. Honest, I'm not. It's time to read to Sister Luke and there are a whole lot of new papers. Magazines, too.'

'She isn't your mother. She's your stepmother.'

He gathers up the newspapers and hugs them against his chest. 'Yes, Sister. I know that.'

* * *

He is now second in the class for spelling, and his reading has come along in leaps and bounds, according to Mrs Rawlins. Leaps and bounds. He likes that. He feels the enthusiasm of words dancing on paper, sentences so full of energy that it is only their full stops that stop them from spilling off the pages. He particularly likes long words that have a string of sounds to them – *residential, comprehensive* – and important names like *Commission of Inquiry* or *Clerical Workers' Union*. Last night, Sister Agnes helped him read a summary of November weather to Sister Luke, and he discovered that the wind which tries to blow his bicycle backwards is called an equinoctial gale. *Equinoctial*. He puts it in his creative writing book and Mrs Rawlins writes EX in red pencil in the margin.

The equinoctial gales are still galing too hard for him to ride up the convent hill. He has to push the bike in gritty air that punches trees and tosses their leaves and twigs across the road. He can't be late. He has stepped into the order of the convent and every afternoon at 3.30 they are waiting for him, his job for the day, pikelets or scones on a plate, cup ready for his cocoa, and the newspaper for Sister Luke.

Police Plant Shell. Police fabrication of evidence is a major finding of the Thomas Royal Commission of Inquiry in its 125-page report tabled in Parliament today.

Twenty-eight-year-old British pilot Judith Chisholm arrived at Auckland tonight to be greeted by pioneer aviator 70-year-old Jean Batten whose flight record Miss Chisholm has just broken.

All retail shops, including butchers, have been given the green light by their workers to open Saturdays unrestricted until Christmas.

'Well done, Brian Collins,' says Mrs Rawlins after school morning report. 'You show the rest of us that there is more to news than a dead canary or an outbreak of measles in the house, but how would you like to put the news into your own words?'

No. He doesn't want to do that. Newspaper words have an authority of their own like soldiers on parade. His own words would make important announcements seem ordinary.

An income tax cut of 5.5 per cent on average to be applied from February 1 next year, highlighted a package of financial measures announced in Parliament last night by the Prime Minister and Minister of Finance, Mr Muldoon.

The country has been buffeted by widespread equinoctial gales which may continue to the end of January, according to forecasts from the Weather Bureau.

Beyond the equinoctial flapping of his shirt and hair, and the equinoctial struggle with his bicycle, he sees the grey car parked outside the convent gate. It's a new Mitsubishi, paintwork mirror-bright, and as far as he knows it doesn't belong to anyone in the parish. He edges his bike around it, noting a black jacket across the back seat, maybe a priest's, and a box of peppermints by the gear stick. He lets the wind slam the gate shut.

There is no one in the kitchen or the dining room, but from the front lounge comes the buzz of voices, some deep and male. He puts his school bag in his room and sits on his bed for a while, waiting for whoever it is to go, but the talk goes on and on, like the drone of a distant aeroplane, and he thinks maybe it'll be all right for him to go to the door to ask if he can get them some tea or something.

They already have tea and Sister Mary Clare is pouring more for Father Fissenden, the new priest at the Cathedral. The other man he knows as Bishop Chaytor, tall even when he's sitting down, his thatch of white hair sticking up like a rooster's comb. They stop talking when Brian appears in the doorway and Bishop Chaytor looks at him over the top of his half-moon glasses. 'So this is the boy?'

He has never spoken to the bishop before and doesn't know what is expected of him. To be on the safe side, he genuflects and says, 'Yes, my Lord.'

'Bishop Bill will do, boy. What's your name?'

'Brian Collins, Bishop – sir. I just – I wanted to know if there was anything –' Everyone is watching him, and he loses the words.

Sister Mary Clare says, 'You can be weeding the path, Brian. We'll tell you when we've finished.'

There is something strange in Sister Mary Clare's voice, something different about all three Sisters, although he doesn't know what it is. The room feels as though everything in it has grown sharp edges. He takes two steps backwards.

'How old are you, Brian?' the bishop says.

'Nine in two months.' He steps back again.

'You're a fine big lad for nine,' says Bishop Chaytor. 'Well, we won't keep you.'

He knows then that they've come about him. He's going to be sent away.

He doesn't weed the path but lies on his bed, door closed to block off the voices. Kids don't live in convents. He's always known that. His father told him he was staying with the Sisters only because there was no one to say otherwise, but his father is wrong. Bishop Chaytor says otherwise.

So now he has to leave. Just as he's learned to skate the full length of the upstairs hall without wobbling, just as he's grown to like the Elvis blanket and can read the newspaper without mixing up the words, just as he's got used to thinking of the convent as his own place, they are going to send him back to his father and the woman who is now Mrs Collins. He curls up, his face into his pillow while the wind blows great equinoctial gusts against the other side of the wall, rattling the loose downpipe the way a dog shakes a rat. The bishop is the voice of the pope and the pope is the voice of God who is too busy to worry about Brian Collins. There is nothing to be done, and although the wishing of it is a sin, he wants to die to be with his mother.

***

He wakes to find the wind turned yellow with sunset outside his high small window, and the bedroom door wide open. He goes into the bathroom, pees and then stands on the toilet to see through the gap in the wooden louvres. The Mitsubishi has gone. He washes his hands, dries them on his hair and readies himself for the bad news.

They are sitting at the kitchen table, hands in laps, not talking, and he thinks that both Sister Mary Clare and Sister Luke have been crying. Either that or the wind has blown dust in their eyes. Through his concern, he wonders if blind eyes feel dust differently from seeing ones. He sits in the fourth place at the table, folds his hands and looks from one to the other. No one says anything. He says it for them.

'I have to leave, don't I?'

Sister Luke nods. 'Yes, Brian.'

Sister Mary Clare makes a funny squeaking noise and gets her handkerchief from her sleeves. She blows her nose, then takes off her glasses to wipe her eyes.

Sister Agnes says, 'We all have to leave, Brian. The bishop is selling the convent.'

He waits for them to say more. They don't. He has to ask, 'Where are we going?'

'There'll be no great change for you, Brian,' says Sister Agnes. 'You'll go home a few weeks early, that's all. As for Sister Luke, Sister Mary Clare and myself, we're going to live with some Sisters in another convent.'

'You've got another convent?' he asks, hope rising like a butterfly.

'No,' says Sister Luke. 'These are Mercy Sisters who are offering us accommodation.'

He tries, 'Can I go there with you?'

Sister Agnes shakes her head.

'But I want to go with you!'

Sister Luke tucks her hands into her sleeves and slowly turns her pink-rimmed eyes his way. 'Bishop Chaytor is quite correct. This

59

house is in poor repair and not worth renovation even if we could find the money. We have known for years that this day would come. The fall of the temple. The serpent on the rock.'

'I can fix things.' He leans forward. 'Did you tell the bishop how good I am at fixing things? Did he see the lawns? Dad'll help me. We'll get everything fixed up and then it won't get sold.'

Sister Mary Clare smiles. 'God bless the boy.'

'It has to be sold,' says Sister Luke. 'It is time.'

'But how do you know you'll like the new convent?' he says.

'More to the point,' says Sister Agnes, 'how will the Mercy Sisters enjoy the invasion from another congregation? I think their offer is extremely generous. I hope it came from them and was not the inspiration of Bishop Chaytor.'

Sister Mary Clare puts her hand over Brian's. 'Scripture is after telling us Himself had no place to lay His head. He'll be looking out for us all, so don't be worrying yourself.'

'When's it getting sold?' he asks.

'We've asked to stay until the end of the year,' says Sister Agnes. 'But it will probably go on the market just as soon as we find the title deeds.' She touches Sister Luke's arm. 'Sister, do you remember where we put the papers?'

'In the –' Sister Luke creases her forehead. 'The Stations of the Cross.'

'Luke, the title deeds.'

'Oberammergau,' says Sister Luke. 'He turned the water into wine.'

'Don't worry,' Sister Agnes tells her. 'They'll be somewhere.'

Brian looks at them and knows they feel as he did when he came home after his mother's funeral. No amount of tea and cakes and hugs could fill the emptiness. 'We can pray for a miracle,' he says. 'St Joseph might stop the convent from getting sold and we can stay.'

'Brian, love,' says Sister Mary Clare. 'If it could change and it wasn't being sold, praise God, you'd still be going back to your Da. His Lordship was awful clear about you being home with your family.'

'But if there is a miracle,' he says, 'a really, really gigantic miracle, he might tell us we can all stay here.' He looks at them. 'Don't you think?'

Sister Agnes smiles at him and shakes her head. 'The miracle will be if we can find the deeds,' she says.

'No one knows where they are at all,' says Sister Mary Clare.

'Or perhaps the miracle will be one of surrender to God's will,' Sister Agnes continues. 'As Gerard Manley Hopkins said, And you unhouse and house the Lord.'

'The world is too much with us,' says Sister Luke. 'The grass withereth. The flower fadeth. The bread of adversity on the waters of affliction.'

'It's too late for the stew,' Sister Mary Clare tells them. 'Would some macaroni cheese do instead? I can boil some potatoes, if you like. Oh look, it's after seven of the clock.'

'Don't fret about it, Brian,' says Sister Agnes. 'It'll work out. Things always do.'

CHAPTER SIX

AT TEN THAT NIGHT BRIAN IS IN THE CANDLE-WASHED chapel, sitting between Sister Luke and Sister Mary Clare, who seem to have forgotten that it is long past his bedtime. The recitation of evening prayer is over and there is a silence as heavy as a big old rock sitting in the candlelit room. This silence, he realises, this heavy thing, is the sale of the convent being offered up to God. The Sisters are not praying for a miracle. They are praying for strength to carry their cross.

Brian already has a list of crosses as long as his arm, his mother's death, Liz Fletcher now Liz Collins, his sister Kathy who keeps telling him he's a spoiled brat, Matthew Cuttance who talks like an atheist and Father Friel who says Brian shouldn't be coming to confession so often because he's making too much of a good thing. How could a good thing be too much? Was it possible that Father Friel didn't believe in miracles? Brian thinks that atheism can happen when God gets too busy to look after his own people. Right now, God seems as far away as the satellites that hurry across the night sky and Brian, with too many burdens of his own to even think about the convent sold, knows there has to be a miracle. It would be easy for God. He'd just have to get off his golden throne for two seconds, a nothing bit of eternity, raise his arm like a wand and *pow*, the convent could be new again, no leaky roof, and Sister Luke could see again and maybe that Liz woman – he stops the thought right there. He was going to say, maybe Liz could go to heaven, too, but a prayer like that would be a sin because it would make his father unhappy again. He has to keep his prayer for a miracle strictly to the convent.

He leans over to scratch his leg, his eyes sliding under lowered lids to see if any of the Sisters are looking his way. Their framed faces are turned towards the tabernacle, and they are sitting as still as statues, except for the small movement of Sister Luke's fingers on her rosary beads. Every now and then Sister Mary Clare lets out a long breath that makes one of the candles flutter.

Well, he'll just have to do it on his own. The miracle prayer. With God being too busy, he'll hand it over to the patron saint of Brian Collins who's fixed the lawnmower and given him the roller-skates. Those miracles did come from his mother. Who else in heaven could influence his Dad to mend the mower? Who else knew that Kathy wouldn't lend him her skates? When she was alive his mother always found a way to fix things in the family without causing too much of a fuss. Now, with her being a saint in heaven, her power would be greater even than Superman's. While God sat on his gold throne talking to the popes about important things, Mum would be around the back in the kitchen, having a cup of tea with Our Lady and her Son. The tea-set would be a lot better than the one Liz was using at home, gold, probably, solid gold with diamonds on the handles of the teacups, and Mum would have made Jesus and his mother some of her date scones. 'You know my son Brian,' she would be saying, 'he wants me to ask you something.'

'A miracle,' he prays under his breath. He pushes all his thinking, his wishing, all his energy, into the prayer. 'Please, Mum, please, a miracle for the nuns and the convent.'

* * *

63

It's Saturday and they've let him sleep in. When he wakes a few minutes before ten, he finds that they've already been to morning Mass and are preparing the breakfast. He looks at three sets of glinting spectacles and he wonders about their crosses. They have no heaviness today. Their quietness is back, not the heavy rock silence but the calm of sunlight in a still room. They don't look happy, but they don't look sad either, as they talk about deeds and transfer documents.

He helps Sister Mary Clare set the table for breakfast. 'What'll happen to the convent, Sister?'

'I'm picking the building'll be pulled down. It's not worth a lot of fixing. The Church'll be building houses for poor families, count on it. For the longest time there's been talk of that.'

'When will you have to go?'

'I don't rightly know to the moment, but you can be sure it won't be before January. The bishop's celebrating Himself's birth in the Holy Land with a fine big Mass at Bethlehem. The papers, though, we have to find those before he comes back. Blessed St Joseph come to our aid, they could be anywhere, even lost. No one's laid an eye on them in thirty years.'

'Mother Magdala's chest,' Sister Luke says suddenly.

The words run through Brian like an electric shock. He doesn't look at Sister Luke but rubs the bowl of a spoon over and over with the tea towel. Of course nuns have chests. Sister Mary Clare's looks like a full shopping bag under her habit. But no one, not even Matthew Cuttance, mentions nuns' chests out loud. This is a problem that people have when they get holes in their brains. The right words fall in the hole and when they reach in to drag them out, they sometimes get the wrong ones.

'In Magdala's chest,' says Sister Luke.

'The grand question being,' says Sister Mary Clare, 'where is Mother Magdala's chest?'

Brian lays the spoon carefully on the table. Perhaps it's all right. Perhaps they are talking about some kind of pirate chest. He looks at Sister Mary Clare.

She gives him the marmalade dish. 'Brian, our first Mother Superior in this convent, God bless her, she brought the Sisters out on a ship from Ireland and on that ship, she was after carrying the sacred items in the most beautiful wooden chest. There were the statues, the books of Rules and Formation. What else? The tabernacle made by an Irish silversmith, and the monstrance, the candlesticks, lovely things like that.'

'It was in the piano room,' says Sister Luke. 'Magdala's chest was always in the corner by the piano. Someone moved it.'

Sister Mary Clare licks the marmalade spoon and rinses it under the tap. 'Sister, dear, it was moved and moved again. Would you be remembering when we had the wallpapering done? Everyone tripping over Mother Magdala's chest and Mother Therese blessing it to high heaven. I don't remember seeing it at all after the wallpapering, I really don't.'

'I'm a trustee,' says Sister Luke. 'Agnes is the other trustee. We have to sign the documents.'

Brian looks quickly at Sister Luke's eyes, pale as skim milk behind her glasses.

Sister Mary Clare says to him, 'To be sure Sister Luke still writes a beautiful hand when she knows where to place the pen. St Joseph will help us and so will our young Brian. We'll not forget Brian now, will we, Sister Luke? He'll be finding the chest, no trouble at all.'

The porridge is cooked. The toast is ready. Sister Agnes comes slowly down the stairs, holding the bannister rail. 'It's not there,' she says.

'The hall cupboard,' says Sister Luke.

'Not in the hall cupboard, nor in any of the cells. I've searched from top to bottom. It simply isn't here.'

Brian wonders if this is the miracle, his mother whisking the chest and the papers up to heaven while they were all sleeping. 'If you can't find the papers, Sister, does that mean the convent can't get sold?'

'No,' says Sister Agnes. 'It means a delay while we get new papers.'

'And where would we be getting those?' asks Sister Mary Clare.

'I'm not sure.' Sister Agnes sits at the table and unfolds her napkin. 'Bishop Bill did say but I don't remember. We'll ask Father Friel. Now let's bow our heads and ask God's blessing.'

* * *

The day is equinoctial again with clouds running like chimney smoke and the loose downpipe clanging on the wall near Brian's room. He thinks he might be able to tie it with some string but there is nothing to tie it to. The loopy bits of tin that once held it in place have broken and the downpipe, full of rust holes, will break too, with all this banging against the weatherboards. It doesn't matter. If his mother gets him his miracle, the convent will be made new. It will dazzle everyone with its brand spanking newness and the bishop will be so impressed he'll never mention selling it again.

He leaves the downpipe and the wind which is throwing bits of foam off the sea and onto the lawn, and goes into the garage to help Sister Mary Clare look for Mother Magdala's chest. The garage is not tidy like the convent. People from the St John Chrysostem youth group store their gear higgledy-piggledy and Brian and Sister Mary Clare have to move kayaks and a ping-pong table just to get in. At the far end there are some wooden racks piled up with cardboard boxes but most of those, too, belong to the youth group. Sister Mary Clare finds some folding chairs she's forgotten they had, and Brian discovers at the back of a shelf a big blue and green glass marble that belongs to nobody.

'Look!' he says. 'A taw!'

'What do you call it now?' asks Sister Mary Clare, looking through cups and saucers in a box.

'A taw, Sister. They're the big marbles you try to win.'

'A taw, you say. To be sure, when we were young, it was the pope's glass eye, and we played in the mud at the back of the schoolhouse, my sisters and brothers and me, and my sister Francie,

66

now there's the one, oh, she had the devilment in her. When I won her pope's eye fair and square, her language was enough to send the Presbyterians running for their rosary beads.' She straightens and puts her hands in the small of her back. 'God never gave me the gift of bending.'

'Does your sister Francie live in Ireland or New Zealand?' he asks.

'Heaven,' she says.

'Heaven,' he echoes, taking in all that the single word implies. 'Like my mother.' Then he says, 'Sister, is it true there are only saints in heaven?'

'Sure and it's true. Don't they teach you anything at school?'

'What about purgatory?'

'What about it?'

'What's it like?'

'Well now, as my mother used to say, it's a place of second chance where you do the homework you didn't get finished in life school.'

He doesn't understand. He tries again. 'Sister, just suppose there was a big earthquake and someone like me got squashed. Would they go to heaven or hell or purgatory?'

'God bless you, Brian, what are you going on about? Is this about you and your dear mother?'

He nods, holding the marble to his eyes and turning it so that his world becomes a flowing river of blue and green. It would be nice to be a pope with a marble for a glass eye but would you be able to see through it?

Sister Mary Clare says, 'For a young lad, it's awful anxious you are. Your lovely mother was an angel even before she went to heaven. You can be sure she'll be up there looking out for you. I told you that before.'

He nods again. 'So I'll see her when I die.'

'Of course you will. Remember what I was after saying about going around to the back of heaven? It'll be your mother all dressed up in the loveliest gown, taking you by the hand to meet Our Lady and Himself, and sure they'll be as pleased as sunshine to see you.'

'Will you and Sister Agnes and Sister Luke be there, too, Sister?'

'By the loving mercy of God so we will. We can have a right party, Brian Collins. Think of all the skating you'll be able to do in heaven.' She bends again to lift the box of china and put it back on the shelf. 'God bless us, the truth is Mother Magdala's wooden box is nowhere in this garage and nowhere in the house. You know what that means, Brian?'

'Nowhere else to look, Sister.'

'So much for our petition to St Joseph. I'm after thinking he's not wanting his convent to be sold and the last of his Sisters sent out to charity.' She takes off her glasses to wipe them and he sees that her eyes are coated with water.

He decides to tell her. 'Sister, I prayed to Mum. I told her to ask Jesus for a miracle.'

She smiles and the wetness runs down from the corners of her eyes. She wipes her cheeks and puts her glasses back on. 'Ah, but that's lovely, Brian. God always hears the prayers of a child.'

He doesn't want to tell her that God on his golden throne didn't even come into his prayer. His petition has gone to the kitchen table at the back of heaven, where his mother is making date scones and Jesus is helping Our Lady to stir the porridge.

'I don't know what we'll do without you,' Sister Mary Clare says.

He rolls the marble between his hands and feels the glass as cold as winter. In his father's Antarctic photos, some ice is bright blue. The true colour of ice, his father told him, is not white but blue, but the human eye can't see blue except in deep cracks where the light strikes at an angle. Maybe, thinks Brian, an albatross sees all ice as blue, the whole of Antarctica shining like a clear sky. Maybe that's how a saint in heaven sees it.

'There'll be a miracle, Sister,' he says. 'It's going to be the biggest miracle anyone's ever seen.' He puts the marble in his pocket. 'Just you wait.'

* * *

In the night he dreams not of an albatross but a huge golden lion that wants to eat him. It makes low growling sounds as it pads towards him through the lavender garden, and its eyes stare straight through him as though he is nothing. He runs inside the convent kitchen and locks the door. It's not just one lock with a key. There are bolts too, a whole row of them from the top of the door to the bottom. While he's pushing them into place he hears a growl at his back. The lion is in the room with him. He doesn't know how it got there. But now the door is locked and he can't escape.

He wakes in the dark, his heart going like a two-stroke motor. He tries to remember the prayer for bad dreams his mother taught him but fear is still crowding words out of his thinking. Yes, yes, he knows it was a dream but he can't get out to put on the light because the lion might be under the bed or in the wardrobe.

He holds the blankets around his neck and listens. The growling noise comes again and this time it's outside his window.

It's not a dream. He's wide awake. The lion is on the other side of the wall and it's making that same I'm-going-to-eat-you sound. Brian throws back his blankets. In one leap he is out of bed, skidding across the lino, out the door and then running for the stairs. The nightlight in the hall throws black shadows long enough to hide the biggest lion. It could be anywhere. He rushes up the stairs, feeling a great whiskery head at his heels. Teeth will close around his ankle. He'll be pulled down into darkness and eaten, bones and pyjamas and all.

He thinks he has Sister Mary Clare's door but as he throws it open he realises his mistake. The 'who's there?' belongs to Sister Agnes.

The light goes on and he blinks at its suddenness. She is sitting up in bed, wearing a white cap that covers her head like a baby's bonnet. Her white nightgown has a high collar and sleeves that come down to her knuckles. 'Brian, what is it?'

'There's a lion – there's –' His breathing sounds like hiccups and he swallows to steady it.

Sister Agnes waves her hand. 'Wait outside.'

'I – I think it got out of a zoo.'

'Go out and close the door,' Sister Agnes says. 'I'll be with you presently.'

He steps back and her bedroom door swings shut, leaving him in the shadows of the hall. He listens. No noise here. The lino, smooth from all his skating and polishing, is cold under his feet. The light is so dim he can barely make out the little holy water fonts outside the bedroom doors. He puts his fingertips into Sister Agnes's font and blesses himself but he has serious doubts that a lion so fierce and hungry is going to be put off by holy water.

When Sister Agnes comes out, she is wearing a thick dressing gown, socks and slippers and her glasses. She still has on the cap tied under her chin. In her hand is a big torch. 'Were you having a nightmare?' she asks.

'Yes, Sister. No. It's real. There's this – this thing outside. I think it's a lion.'

'I very much doubt it, but shall we look?'

Fear drains away like water down a plughole and he follows her down the stairs. 'I'm sorry to wake you up, Sister.'

'It's all right,' she says. 'I wasn't asleep.'

* * *

In the kitchen she makes two cups of sweet milky cocoa because it's good for the nerves, she says, and she describes how the possum was eating the roses outside his window.

'I didn't know they made a noise like that,' he says. 'I thought it was a lion coming to eat me.'

Sister Agnes recites, 'And dar'st thou then to beard the lion in his den? That's Sir Walter Scott.' She smiles. 'Where would a lion come from?'

'God,' he says.

'God?' She puts down her cup.

'Yes, Sister.'

'Why do you think God would be sending a lion after you?'

'The miracle, Sister.' He thinks he should explain. 'I didn't ask God. I prayed around the back of heaven and asked Mum to ask Jesus and Mary. I thought God was wild with me for ignoring him.'

Sister Agnes looks at him over the top of her glasses. 'Is this about the papers in Mother Magdala's chest?'

He shakes his head. 'Oh no, Sister. It's a much much bigger miracle than that. The convent is going to be made brand new and Sister Luke's eyes will get better and the bishop'll be so pleased he'll let me stay here and help you.'

Sister Agnes smiles. 'Ah, but Brian, suppose that's not God's will for us?'

He looks at the skin forming on his cocoa. 'I thought –' He scratches his head. 'I thought that's why God sent the lion. Only it was a possum.'

Sister Agnes doesn't say anything for a long time. In her dressing gown and cap she looks different, more like an old lady than a nun. Or an old man. Like the photos of his grandfather. He can't see any hair under her cap and wonders if it gets sheared like sheep's wool or just cut with scissors. She reaches her left hand across the table towards him and he sees that her gold ring has cotton wound around it to stop it falling off her finger.

'You look just like Grandad,' he says.

'So do you, Brian Collins,' she replies with a small smile.

He doesn't want to look like his grandfather and Sister Agnes. He lifts the skin off his cocoa. 'Mum always said I took after Dad.'

'That's true, but you're more like his father. You're the spitting image of my brother Liam.' She pats him on the shoulder. 'Listen, Brian, I know you're unhappy about your father marrying again. It's eating at you like a worm in an apple. But it's not the first time it's happened in the Collins family. Our mother died in childbirth when I was six and our father remarried. But the woman was not like Elizabeth Fletcher. Indeed, our stepmother had no interest in children at all, and she took our father away from us, right away, across the sea to America. It was my brother Liam, your grandfather, who left his studies at the university and came home to look after his six brothers and sisters. He worked on the railways, ran the home, cooked our meals, knocked our heads together when we were fighting and dragged us all along to Mass on Sundays. Most particularly, he cared about our education, every one of us.'

Brian is remembering his father's family stories. 'Is that why he got married when he was old?' he asks.

'Forty-six isn't all that old,' she says. 'I state as a matter of fact rather than of pride that I was Liam's favourite sibling. He wanted for me all the learning he'd left to raise us and it was he who steered me to university and gave me a loving for Milton and Yeats and Manley Hopkins.' She slowly stands and, with a cup in each hand, walks to the bench. 'When Liam told me he was getting married, I left the university and went into religious life.' She puts the cups in the sink and turns on the tap.

'Was it hard being a nun?' he asks.

'Shall I tell you the hardest thing? Giving up smoking. That's a vivid memory. The day I entered, standing outside the gates and having the last puff of the last cigarette before I went in.'

He tries to imagine Sister Agnes as a young woman smoking, and can't. He says, 'What would you have been if you hadn't been a nun?'

'Oh, probably something the same, a teacher who reads poetry and talks to God. I told you all that, for just one reason, so you could find a little appreciation in your heart for your father's new wife. She's a good woman, Brian.'

He slides down in the chair and says nothing.

'Your father couldn't have got a better woman, if your mother had chosen her herself. Have you thought about that? Might it not be your mother, God bless her, who brought them together?'

He looks at the floor.

'The bishop says you have to go back to your family. I don't think there's any miracle going to get around that, although I see no harm in you staying until the bishop returns from Israel. You know what that means, Brian. Sometime soon you'll need to make your peace with Elizabeth.'

'It's not just Liz,' he mumbles.

'What did you say?'

He begins to cry. 'It's not just Dad and Liz. I – I like living here.'

'Ah Brian!' She puts her hand on his shoulder. 'It was only ever temporary.'

'I don't want to go!'

'None of us wants to go,' she says, 'but it's God's will that counts, not ours. Go to your bed, Brian. If the noise comes back, say a prayer for the rose outside your window.'

* * *

In the morning the convent still has peeling weatherboards and rattling downpipes but there is a hail storm which is a sort of a miracle, a sudden rattle of whiteness against the roof and windows, ice-balls bouncing on the lawn.

'Snow!' he cries.

'I don't think so,' says Sister Luke. 'Snow doesn't make a noise.'

'I mean it looks like snow.' He presses his nose against the window, which is as cold as a fridge door. 'It's all over the grass, Sister, white as white.'

'How deep?'

'I don't know. About three centimetres.'

'Inches,' she says.

He's not sure how to measure in inches. 'Five or six,' he guesses.

'We will need a ride to Mass,' says Sister Luke. 'Please tell Sister Agnes to phone for a ride.'

While they wait for the car, the hail turns to mush and the Sisters tease him about his lion.

'We must be after getting you a donkey's jawbone to keep under your pillow,' chuckles Sister Mary Clare.

'What for?' he asks.

'Samson slew the lion with the jawbone of an ass,' she says.

'Sister, he slew the Philistines,' says Sister Agnes. 'We're not told how he killed the lion.'

'I'm not doubting it's the same jawbone,' says Sister Mary Clare. 'Kept it under his pillow and used it to comb his hair and all.'

'Lion of Judah,' says Sister Luke, shaking her head. 'The world intrudes on us and there's no fish today.' She turns her head towards Sister Mary Clare. 'You say the chest has gone from its keeping.'

'Oh, those papers!' sighs Sister Mary Clare, her smile going behind a cloud.

'I wonder if Patricia would remember,' says Sister Agnes.

'We could be phoning her,' Sister Mary Clare says.

Sister Luke lifts her head quickly. 'Yes, we could,' she says. 'We could call Patricia, God bless her. Patricia will know.'

* * *

Brian holds the doors of Mrs Hennessey's car for them, and then runs ahead down the hill through the puddles towards the church. He arrives at the front steps just as Mrs Hennessey drives up, and is able to open the car doors again. His sisters Kathy and Debbie are standing near the church door and he guesses that Kathy will commit the sin of name-calling as he goes in, but he is already guarding himself from retaliation. If he wants the big miracle, he can't afford to blow it, especially not on someone as stupid – someone as difficult as his eldest sister.

He would like to sit down the front with the nuns but they have made the rule that every Sunday he sits with his family. Kathy and Beth have been waiting to take him inside where Liz and Dad, Nicky and Joey, are already seated under the Fifth Station of the Cross. Kathy doesn't call him names or say anything rotten, but as they kneel at the end of the pew, she whispers, 'The bishop said you had to come home.'

He nods as he blesses himself.

'I'll have to shift out of your room,' Kathy says. 'What a bloody pain.'

He nods again and looks along the row to acknowledge his father and Liz. All right, Brian, he tells himself, smile! Smile at her. Remember the miracle, lean towards it like a starter in a race, miracle, miracle, brand new convent, Sister Luke seeing so she can read the newspaper and the hole in her brain closed over so she can remember what she's read, a miracle like Lourdes or Fatima, that'll knock the bishop for six, please, Mum, please ask them.

He smiles at his father's new wife.

Liz almost drops her church newsletter, then her round face gets rounder and she smiles back. His Dad, watching, looks so pleased that for a moment it seems as though he's going to lean across the girls and say something. Brian closes his eyes and folds his hands.

I did it, he says to his mother. I was nice to her. I hope it's what you wanted.

* * *

The church is in waiting for the birth of Jesus, the Advent candles lit, the crib in the corner smelling of fresh hay. The sense of anticipation is so strong in Brian that he feels the electricity of it in his arms and legs, such a tingling that maybe at this minute the convent is winding back like a video in reverse, to newness. He stands on his toes to see if Sister Luke's eyes have been touched by a miracle but there are too many heads in the way for him to see.

'Advent is the time of preparation,' says Father Friel in his homily, 'a time when we are open to the light of Christ on our lives illuminating what comes from our fears and what comes from love.'

Brian knows that time can go backwards in heaven, too. At Advent, Jesus of the bleeding heart and pierced hands rewinds to become the baby, chuckling and grabbing at Mary's long hair. In the kitchen of heaven, Our Lady sits with Jesus at the table, watching while Brian's mother plays the bear game on Jesus's hand.

Round and round the mulberry bush ran the teddy bear. One step. Two step. Jesus laughs and laughs as Brian's mother tickles him under the arm, and all of heaven shakes with the happiness of it. 'I have a son, too,' says Brian's mother. 'He needs a miracle.'

Brian goes up for Holy Communion behind Kathy, who has green ribbons plaited into her hair. His sister has no respect at all. You'd think she was stuffing a sandwich into her mouth. He stands taller and holds out his hands, exactly cupped to receive the sacred host from Father Friel. He parts his lips, feels the body of Christ dissolving like a snowflake on his tongue.

The Advent choir is singing, 'Love divine all loves excelling, joy of heaven to earth come down.'

He wishes he lived in a country where there was snow at Christmas. He has never seen real thick snow. He thinks that to be in Antarctica must feel like zillions of Holy Communions.

* * *

He runs up the hill before Mrs Hennessey's car can get out of the church parking lot, and flings himself panting at the gate. The miracle hasn't happened yet but it might have started. He thinks the paint is looking a bit brighter under the upstairs windows.

He finds the key under the brick, goes in and starts setting the table for breakfast, getting as far as butter on the butter dish, before they arrive.

Weet-Bix and stewed apple. Sister Mary Clare's marmalade. Don't forget to warm the teapot. The toaster is one of the old kind that doesn't pop and he's learned to get the toast exactly right without burning his fingers.

Sister Luke always wants to know about everyone at Mass and Sister Mary Clare tells her, describing the children and their families, connections that reach out like roots all over the town. Brian turns the bread before the brown can deepen to black and shakes the heat out of his fingertips. He's forgotten the milk. He must pour it into the china jug and put the beaded cover over it.

'Not the High Street Connollys,' says Sister Mary Clare. 'The ones from Jekyll Street. Such a thing, Sister! If it wasn't enough, the poor woman breaking her leg like that.'

'I don't remember any Connollys in Jekyll Street,' says Sister Luke, feeling her way to her chair.

'Well, now, I'm thinking you taught her sister Barbara piano lessons back goodness knows when but I wouldn't be too sure, myself. Brian, love, you'll be starving. Sit down, there's a grand lad. Where's Agnes?'

'The world intrudes,' says Sister Luke. 'It is too much with us.'

'I'm okay,' Brian says to Sister Mary Clare. 'I'll just finish the toast.'

'I don't know,' says Sister Luke, 'why we didn't have a homily today. He's getting very forgetful, isn't he? Is this stewed apple or pear?'

'Sisters!' It's Sister Agnes coming from the front room, running from side to side on her creaky knees. She stops in the doorway. 'Sisters, I've been talking to Patricia. She says the chest is in the attic.'

* * *

Only Brian can climb the ladder. Sister Mary Clare and Sister Agnes help him carry the wooden stepladder up the stairs. They prop it under the trapdoor in the hall and hold it steady while he climbs. This is not like the garage roof. There is no wall to hold. He must climb all the way to the second rung from the top and then try to push open the door in the ceiling, which is no bigger than the lid of a washing machine. His legs wobble and he pauses for a moment, looking down at Sister Luke, who is feeling her way along the wall. What if she bumps into them?

'Let me help you, Sister,' says Sister Mary Clare, reaching out to her.

Now all three are holding the ladder and he's got one hand resting against the white painted ceiling, the other pushing the trapdoor. It lifts so easily that he almost loses his balance.

'Careful now,' says Sister Luke, her cloudy eyes turned up towards the ceiling. 'You don't have wings yet, Brian Collins.'

'Sure and we would catch you,' says Sister Mary Clare. 'That's a mighty dark hole that is. Holy Mother protect us. Sisters, are you thinking the lion could be hiding up there.'

Their laughter is like the rattling of spoons in tea cups.

'Oh, don't tease the lad,' says Sister Luke.

'Here's some light on the subject,' says Sister Agnes, standing on her toes to pass him her torch. 'You'll need to get up in the ceiling, Brian. Put the torch up and then yourself and mind how you go.'

With his hands on the edge of the hole, he lifts himself until he is seated with his legs dangling above their heads. He picks up the torch and waves it around. No wonder the roof leaks. The iron has holes that look like stars and there is a wet smell up there like mushrooms and old potatoes, although he sees only cobwebs. He directs the torch beam nearer to where he is sitting and sees a dusty wooden box with something like carving on the lid.

'I think I've found it!' he calls.

'Thank you, St Joseph!' says Sister Mary Clare. 'Thank you, Patricia. Thank you, Brian Collins.'

'The world intrudes,' says Sister Luke. 'There is no justice for the wicked.'

* * *

Father Friel comes to tea and brings a black jersey that needs darning at the elbows. 'I hear you had a visit from Bishop Bill,' he says, poking his fingers through the holes in the sleeves. 'How's your mending basket, Mary Clare?'

Sister Mary Clare pretends to be cross. 'I never did see a man so awful hard on clothes,' she says, snatching at the jersey, which smells of pipe tobacco.

'News travels with such speed,' says Sister Agnes. 'Remember Milton? Evil news rides post while good news baits.'

'You're the only person I know who remembers Milton,' says Father Friel, taking off his jacket. As he drapes it over the back of the chair, something crackles and he pushes his hand into an inside pocket. 'Here, Collins. A bag of anti-worry tablets.' He half-pushes, half-throws a cellophane pack of liquorice allsorts at Brian, who catches them with hands full of tablecloth.

'Gee, thank you, Father! Choice!'

'What are you doing?' Father Friel nods at the cloth.

'Setting the table, Father.'

'You should be out kicking a ball around.'

'He does that too,' says Sister Mary Clare, 'but it'll be doing him no harm at all to know how to lay a table.'

'God bless him,' says Sister Luke. 'Where would we be without our Brian.'

Brian avoids Father Friel's swivelling eyes and steps around him to put the cloth on the table.

'It won't be for much longer,' says Father Friel.

'He's a wonder,' says Sister Luke. 'Even keeps the lions out of the roses.'

The Sisters smile but do not explain the joke to Father Friel, who is tapping on the table as though he is typing. 'Bishop phoned,' he says. 'Said I had to get in touch with his father.'

'Well, now, I'm sure he can stay until the bishop gets back from the Holy Land,' says Sister Mary Clare, bringing her sewing basket in from the laundry.

'That's not exactly what his Lordship said.' Father Friel's eyes flicker towards Sister Agnes. 'I didn't know Joe Collins was your nephew.'

Sister Agnes nods slightly. 'Did the bishop tell you he's selling the convent?'

'No. I heard about that from Kevin Frissenden.'

'Until this afternoon, we thought we'd lost the deeds,' says Sister Mary Clare. 'You wouldn't believe the search we had. They were all the time in Mother Magdala's chest up in the attic.'

'We have to get transfer documents,' says Sister Agnes. 'I'm not sure how we should do that. I thought you might be able to advise us.'

'Have you got a lawyer?' asks Father Friel.

Sister Agnes smiles. 'What would we do with a lawyer?'

'You should have one,' he says.

'The diocese has a firm of solicitors,' says Sister Agnes. 'Bishop Chaytor says they'll take care of the actual transfer. All we have to do is sign. But he did tell us to procure the documentation for the transfer.'

'You ask for my advice? My advice is get a lawyer,' says Father Friel.

'He wants everything ready for his return,' Sister Agnes says.

Brian moves around the bulk of Father Friel to place a knife and spoon. The afternoon sun is streaming through the window and the butter on the table is melting like snow.

'If I were you, I wouldn't worry about the papers,' says Father Friel. 'Loveridge has been after this property for months. A week or two is not going to affect the sale. The best thing I can tell you now is consult a lawyer.'

'Loveridge,' says Sister Agnes.

'Would that by chance be Mr Matthew Loveridge?' asks Sister Mary Clare, threading a needle with black wool.

'His Lordship didn't tell you?' Father Friel looks at them with his big fish eyes.

'Poor man,' says Sister Luke. 'His daughter had measles and her baby was born stone deaf.'

'Loveridge,' Sister Agnes says again.

Father Friel's eyes go quick, quick, around the table. 'Three hundred thousand,' he says. 'Almost a third of a million dollars for an acre of land and a building that needs demolishing. Hmm? No wonder Bill's rubbing his hands together. Money for the cathedral fund. Ha! Word is, Loveridge'll be building a restaurant and motel units.' He picks up a knife and taps it on the table. 'I'm telling you this in confidence, of course.'

'Of course,' says Sister Agnes.

'Cathedral rumour,' he says. 'Reliable, but still rumour. I'm sure the bishop will fill you in with the details.'

'I'm sure,' says Sister Agnes. 'If you'll excuse me, I should heat the soup.'

'Three hundred thousand,' says Father Friel and gives a long soft whistle.

Sister Mary Clare draws a long black thread through the sleeve of the jersey. 'Blessed St Joseph, would you think of such a thing? Motels and a restaurant.'

Sister Luke turns her head towards Father Friel. 'Brian found Pandora's chest,' she says. 'It was in the attic and Agnes has made your favourite soup.'

'What kind?' Father Friel ask Sister Agnes.

She replies, 'Bacon hock and pea with soda bread.'

'Ah but that's grand.' Father Friel sits back and locks his fingers over his stomach. 'Don't forget the legal advice,' he says. 'It is your convent, you know.'

Brian slides the breadboard and knife onto the table and smiles inside himself at the talk of lawyers and motels. He imagines the look on their faces when the miracle takes place. The brand new convent will become a holy shrine, thousands of visitors kneeling to see visions of Our Lady with Brian Collins's mother right beside her above the new iron roof. Two mothers standing in shining robes, their hands outstretched to the world. They will smile at each other as mothers do, and Our Lady will ask Brian's mother to bring her the prayers of the faithful, especially the three holy nuns who will be in front of the crowd. Sister Mary Clare won't get tired so easy, Sister Agnes will have knees that kneel without hurting and Sister Luke won't even need her glasses to see it all.

CHAPTER SEVEN

EVERYONE KNOWS THAT THE BISHOP WANTS TO SELL THE convent and Brian's uncles are saying it's about time, the old building is an eyesore, getting so dangerous with the rain coming in, it's a wonder the good Sisters haven't been electrocuted.

'I've checked their wiring,' says Brian's father.

'It's not your responsibility,' says Aunty Deb. 'You do enough for them, God only knows.' She pauses. 'You and young Brian. Good thing he'll be out of there.'

Brian's Dad rips the top off another can of beer. 'I don't know about that. It's been a bit of a haven for him, you know. He was very close to his mother.'

'It's not what I'd want for any boy of mine,' growls Uncle Denny.

'Brian is Brian,' says Dad. 'He's different. Who's to say that's a bad thing? I try, Denny, God knows I try, to do the best for all my kids and I must say, with Brian –' His voice trails off as though he is shaking his head.

'You're soft, Joe, that's your problem. Sometimes the best medicine for a kid is a good clip over the earhole. You could have had him sorted out months ago and saved yourself a lot of trouble.'

Brian, pressed against the wall outside the door, hears his father laugh and feels betrayal. Uncle Denny is – is –. He stops himself. Uncle Denny is Mum's brother but he's as much like her as a snake is like a dove.

'Are they going to demolish it or what?' asks Aunty Anne. 'Some of that old timber is beautiful, the stairs, the panelling in the chapel. I wouldn't mind getting those stairs before they knock it down.'

'I think you can be sure that anything like that will be sold,' says Brian's father. 'Can I get anyone another gin?'

Brian hears him pick up glasses. He quickly turns away from the door and goes to the kitchen, where Liz is putting Christmas cake on a glass dish. The gold band on her finger glows with newness. 'I've made two cakes,' she tells him. 'One for before Christmas and one for after. Would you like some?'

He shakes his head, then, remembering his new promise, he takes a small piece from the edge of the dish and nibbles at it.

'It's got pineapple in it,' says Liz. 'And nuts and raisins and figs, but I suppose you're not all that interested in Christmas cake recipes. You probably don't even like Christmas cake.'

He nibbles again. 'It's all right.'

'Thanks.' She smiles. 'Thanks for trying.'

He shrugs and has another nibble. She is right. He doesn't like Christmas cake.

'Only another week of school and you'll be home,' she says. 'We're looking forward to it, Brian. Your father's missed you. You're his right-hand man. He often says how lucky the nuns are to have you.'

Brian knows this is soft-talk and probably all untrue but he has made a solemn promise to his mother that he will stop giving Liz a hard time. So far, he has kept his side of the bargain but the miracle hasn't happened, and he now wonders if he asked too much. He wishes he could talk to an expert in miracles who could put him right about the dos and don'ts of asking. It could be like Christmas. You get about half the things you put on your list. But the difficulty is he hasn't received even half of what he's wanted.

Sister Mary Clare was not much help. Miracles, she told him, are everywhere. Tell me, she said, of one thing that is not a miracle.

'Would you like new curtains for your room?' asks Liz.

He shakes his head.

'I could make them.' She is smiling more than is necessary. 'You could choose the material.'

'No.'

She goes on, not understanding a single blessed thing. 'I want to make sure you like them. Heck, I couldn't bear having curtains I didn't like. I saw some material with penguins –'

'Get what you like,' he says. 'It doesn't matter. Honest, it doesn't.' He says the rest in his head. Because I'm not coming back. Not never, ever. I don't belong in this house.

* * *

He knows other families who go out on Sunday afternoons, to the beach, go-cart racing, movies, swimming pool. His family has never done that, not even when Mum was alive. The relatives all go to each other's houses, mostly Joe Collins's place because he's got more room, and the entire afternoon is wasted away with the adults sitting around yakking and drinking beer while the kids play outside or watch videos. Brian doesn't like his cousins all that much. Not that he dislikes them. It's just that they seem to live on another planet. Cousin Lucinda, who is one month younger than Brian, wants a Cabbage Patch doll for Christmas. Her brother Paddy, twelve and as long and skinny as a flagpole, has only one ambition, to look sixteen to see the film *Apocalypse Now*. Nobody cares that children in Africa are starving to death or that the convent is being sold. Nobody believes in miracles.

Paddy looks hard at Brian and says, 'My father reckons nuns are bad luck.'

84

'They are not!'

'Yes, they are. Like witches. You walk in their shadow and you'd better watch out.'

'That's not true!' he says. 'That's blasphemery.'

'You mean blasphemy. And it ain't a lie, Brian Collins. Walk in a nun's shadow and you'll get all your words mixed up.'

The others laugh, siding with Paddy, and Brian understands what Sister Luke means when she says, 'The world is too much with us.' The world is the place of Cabbage Patch dolls, blasphemery and new curtains, while he, Brian Collins, belongs in the world of miracles at the convent. He knows the truth of this. He can feel goodness in his heart, shining like a sanctuary lamp, and he is convinced that his efforts to be nice to Liz are making a difference. He tells his cousins it's a sin to tell lies about nuns, and when Paddy, who likes movies about war and blood, calls him a pious twit, he smiles, knowing that all the saints have been given a hard time. That's the cost of miracles.

He goes to the corner of the sunporch where his father has a desk with a typewriter and adding machine, and he pulls from one of the bookshelves above it a photo album full of pictures of his father, with a beard snowcrusted like a Christmas tree, in a field of white that goes on for ever. He turns a page. His father is crouching in the whiteness, in front of a penguin that has its head thrust forward, its wings spread. Penguins, said his father, fly under water. Penguins have long leg bones but their bodies come down to their ankles like sleeping bags, which is why they waddle. You could write a stack of books about penguins, his father said. But it is the snow that always brings Brian back to the photographs. He looks at a yellow tractor which has left marks like long fancy ribbons in the whiteness. In the background is a snow-covered mountain with white clouds like feathers stuck on its peak, the hat of a ghostly pirate. He touches the smoothness of the photo, imagining texture. It can be like sugar underfoot, said his father, or sand, or slippery as oil or hard as rock. It depends. And cold? Brian asked. His father laughed. Of course it's cold, you daft beggar. But Brian wasn't asking a simple question. He always wants to know the size of coldness, how wide, how deep, how for ever the beard-crusting, finger-breaking, lung-cutting cold of Antarctic snow. He turns the pages backwards. At the South Pole, said his father, there is this funny round hut. Inside the hut there are separate rooms like little boxes. Open a box and in it are people drinking coffee and watching a video. The world is too much with us in Antarctica. Brian turns pages, more people, more penguins, fuel drums, his father standing by a helicopter, everyone fat with clothing thick as moon suits, black sunglasses holding perfect reflections of glaciers, another lot of penguins, and back to the first page of the album where his mother in a blue dress and his father without a beard are standing by the flowering cherry tree, with their arms around each other, smooching. Brian himself, then only six, took the photo with Dad's new camera, the week before Dad went south. Dad set the camera on a tripod, lined it up and put Brian's finger on the button. Push when I tell you. Brian remembers the quickness of his mother's face and the sound of her laughter when her father said 'Now!' in the middle of a kiss, a kiss that would last for ever.

A thought sharp as a needle suggests he leaves the album open at this page, on Liz's side of the new double bed in the next room. He feels bright pleasure and then alarm at the strength of the suggestion. The light in his heart is reduced to a pale flicker and he tells himself it must be the devil trying to spoil the goodness of his prayers for a miracle. He's not sure about the devil since Sister Mary Clare told him Satan might be just another name for the things people are afraid of in themselves, but he is concerned that the temptation to hurt Liz should erupt like a firecracker in the middle of his efforts to be nice. He crosses himself in front of his mother's picture, closes the album, puts it back on the shelf and goes back to the kitchen, where Liz is drying dishes.

He says, 'I don't need new curtains because I'm staying at the convent.'

She looks at him but doesn't say anything.

'I'm praying for a miracle,' he says. 'It's going to happen. I have to tell you, it's not you. It's – it's – they need me to help them. The convent won't get sold.'

She doesn't laugh like Father Friel nor is she like Sister Agnes, telling him he must bow to God's will. She puts the tea towel on the bench and sits in the chair opposite. Her eyes are blue with black pencil lines that make her look like a panda bear. 'That's nice, Brian.'

'Miracles are real,' he tells her.

'That's what I believe too,' she says.

So then he tells her the rest of it, his prayers for everything being made new, the building, Sister Luke, Sister Agnes's creaky bones, the convent becoming a holy place for pilgrims, like Lourdes. Finally, he tells her about his patron saint.

She nods. 'If anyone has influence, it's your mother. She was a wonderful woman.'

He is surprised and a little embarrassed that he has said so much. But it's all right. She doesn't laugh. He puts his foot on the edge of his chair and picks at a blue toenail that happened when his skates ran into a skirting board by Sister Agnes's room. He says, 'That time I said you weren't my mother –'

'I know.'

'I didn't mean –'

'I'm not,' she says. 'I never will be. People have only got one mother.'

He feels relief. 'You're my stepmother.'

'No,' she says. 'I definitely don't want to be a stepmother.'

'What are you then?'

'I don't know.' She folds the tea towel, smoothing it on her knee. 'Whatever you like. Maybe just Liz.' She smiles at him quickly, looks back at the towel. 'I suppose what I'd really like is to be your friend.'

He can't answer that. It's too hard. He scrapes away some of the black stuff under the toenail.

'If the miracle doesn't, you know, work out the way you want it, you can still get new curtains.'

'Okay,' he says. 'Not penguins.'

'Whatever you like.' She looks at the tea towel which she has folded into a small thick square. 'There are simply terrible kids' stories about stepmothers,' she says.

* * *

Scrup, scrupo. Brian tries to remember the name of the disease that might already be in his blood, an angry germ laying eggs in the walls of his heart. It's a long name. He couldn't ask his father to repeat it, because he was doing his usual thing, listening behind the door while his father talked to the adults. Scroopy something, caught in old convents with leaking roofs and probably like chicken-pox only much rarer. He coughs in front of the small mirror in his room, and mists his reflection. No, he doesn't have a cold. He doesn't have a headache or itchy spots.

He asks the Sisters. 'What is scroopy – scrup – you know.'

Sister Agnes puts a finger on her book and looks up. 'Scroopy?'

'Yes, Sister.'

'I haven't the faintest idea.'

Sister Mary Clare doesn't stop knitting. 'Is it after being some kind of new game?'

'No, Sister. It's – it's like measles. I thought you'd know about it.'

'Why would we know, Brian?' asks Sister Agnes.

'Because you catch it in convents.'

Sister Agnes's smile is as thin as string. 'School talk,' she says.

He shakes his head. 'Father Friel,' he tells her. 'He told Dad and Dad told my Aunty Deb. Father Friel reckoned I'd get a bad dose of it if I stayed at the convent.'

'Scroopy?' says Sister Agnes, now frowning.

Sister Luke stirs in her armchair. She waves a hand. 'Scrupulosity.'

'That's it!' he says. 'Scrupolos – scrupoty.'

Sister Agnes looks at Sister Mary Clare and her mouth twitches as though she is going to cry. 'Scrupulosity,' she says slowly.

Sister Mary Clare stabs a needle into a stitch. 'Sure and that's a nothing kind of word to be passing around the parish, not worth the sound it makes.'

'Have you had it?' he asks.

'Praise God, no!' she laughs. 'At least, not for a long time. It's not something you catch like a sniffle, Brian. In truth, you don't catch it at all.'

'Be assured, Father Friel was mistaken,' says Sister Agnes. 'What did your Dad say about your school report? Was he pleased?'

'I – I think so.'

Sister Luke's hands perch like birds' claws on the arms of her chair. She leans forward, her head turned towards Brian. 'It means excessive piety.'

'Tisha!' says Sister Mary Clare, with a movement that sends her ball of wool rolling across the carpet. 'People who invent words like that have nothing better to do with their brains or time.'

* * *

There isn't much work during the last week of school. Everyone is too busy with report papers, inter-school tennis, choir practice and rehearsals for the school concert. Last year Brian was a wise man in the Advent play. This year he is part of the choir and is one of the angels singing at the back of the stable behind Chris Ryan, who is Joseph, and Moana Taylor, who is Mary. Brian hoped to be Joseph. He thought that living at the convent of St Joseph the Labourer would have some influence, but still, as an angel, he does get to sing a solo verse in 'O Little Town of Bethlehem'. He practises with Sister Agnes at the convent piano until he can breathe in the right places and sing the words without swallowing them. The only trouble is he has to wear the same white gown that was worn by his sister Kathy, who was an angel three years ago.

The miracle hasn't happened.

On Monday and Tuesday Sister Luke and Sister Agnes are in

town with the convent papers and he cuts the lawns while Sister Mary Clare picks runner beans and makes sauce from the early plums that hang like Christmas decorations on the tree by the gate. On Wednesday they are all away and he must let himself in with the key from under the stone. He has with him an Advent candle and candlestick that he has been making at school. He's planned it as a gift for the Sisters, to replace the plain old candles they have on the altar, but he thinks it will do no harm to light it before they come back.

He leaves his sandals in the kitchen and goes barefooted into the hush of the chapel. For a while he stands with his toes curled in the carpet, holding it all to himself, the stained glass window showing St Joseph in a brown apron, a hammer in his hand, assembled like a glowing jigsaw with black edges, and the tabernacle with Jesus locked inside and the red lamp flickering like a beating heart. The statues in front of the chapel are small, Our Lady with her hands held out and St Joseph holding a white flower. Behind them, beneath the stained glass window, is Jesus on the cross, his head bowed in a ring of spiky thistles. Brian once tried that. Last Lent when the hurt of missing his mother got so bad, Sister Agnes told him to talk to Jesus about it. Brian wanted to do more. For some reason he can't remember, he made a circle from some rose prunings and put it on his head, but it made his eyes water and he'd got a thorn in the skin behind his ear. His father prised it out with a needle, telling him that's what he got for playing hide-and-seek in the rose garden.

It feels a bit strange being in the chapel without the holy nuns but this is his chance to be heard. Prayers, he thinks, go up to heaven like smoke and usually there are four lots from the chapel, twisting and twining together. Sister Mary Clare says prayers always get to heaven and he believes that, but the words must take some sorting out, like letters in a post office.

He puts the candle on the altar, and lights it.

The candlestick is a piece of wood painted white with a nail in it to hold the candle, which is red. It sits in a circle of white pine cones, white shells and silver ribbon. The new wick grows a pale flame which climbs higher and sways, making the cones and shells dance against their shadows. He slides down onto a kneeler in front of the candle, folds his hands, and tries to see his mother in its light. 'Please, please,' he whispers. 'They're doing the papers. Please, Mum, hurry before the bishop gets back.'

* * *

They come into the chapel while he is praying. He hears their rustling as they kneel behind him and he smells the liniment Sister Agnes uses for her knees, a scent like incense mixed with cough lollies. That time he came off Martin Cano's skateboard and left skin and blood on the basketball court, he couldn't kneel at Mass for two Sundays. Why does Sister Agnes always kneel? He can hear her pain at his back, a catch in her breath, a clicking in her bones, but she still gets down on the kneeler, slow, slow, crackle, rustle. He hears Sister Luke's beads and Sister Mary Clare's breathing. A miracle, he prays. Please, please, a miracle.

* * *

They're very happy about the candle and Sister Mary Clare tells him they'll light it every Advent for as long as Himself spares them.

Sister Luke says, 'Tell me how you made it.'

He describes every part of the process, sanding the wood, the painting, the glue, and she laughs, her lips lifting away from her old grey teeth. 'Oh those pine woods,' she says. 'The turtle dove is singing in the land.'

'The candle is half paraffin and half beeswax so it smells nice,' he tells her.

Still laughing, she shakes her head. 'Very nice, Brian, paraffin, beeswax, but we need to read the paper. Sisters, do we have the newspaper today? Or did we just make the news?'

'Both, Sister dear.' Sister Mary Clare puts her arm under Sister Luke's hand and guides her towards her chair. 'But Brian won't be after reading to you this very minute. He's getting ready for the school concert and so are we. He's an angel. He's singing in the choir, are you remembering, Luke?'

Sister Luke frowns. 'We already went to the school concert.'

'That was last year,' says Sister Mary Clare. 'This year's will be even better, I'm thinking. This will be the time of rejoicing. Glory to God in the Highest.'

Now even Sister Agnes laughs and Brian, looking from one to another, is delighted that his Advent candle has made them so happy.

* * *

With so much work before Christmas, his father can't come to the school concert, but Liz is there, holding Joey on her hip as though he's her own child, and talking to the Sisters, who are seated in the front row. Brian is sure they are discussing him but he can't hear what they are saying. The hall is full of parents, all of them shouting at the top of their voices. He thinks if kids made this much noise, a teacher would tell them to shut their faces, holy season or no holy season.

Someone taps him on the shoulder. It is Mrs Treadwell, who is producing the play. She holds one of those kite-like contraptions of wire, white paper and tapes. 'Leave the curtain alone, Brian. It's time for your wings.'

As he turns towards her, his shoe gets caught in the hem of his angel gown and he feels rather than hears the tearing of the fabric. He looks down at his stomach and sees grey shirt poking through.

'Heaven help us!' says Mrs Treadwell. 'What is it with boys and hems? You're the third tonight. Pins, Brian. I've got safety pins. Just hurry up and get into position.'

The principal calls on Father Friel to bless the evening and then the Marchant brothers play two piano duets while Joseph and Mary get settled on the hay bale, with the shepherds arranged beside them. The angels line up at the back of the stage, some of them deliberately crashing into each other with their wings. Brian tries to keep to himself, but Tony Ryan comes at him sideways, his own wings in tatters, and next thing a stray wire hooks into Brian's paper feathers.

'Ha ha! Shot you down in flames, Collins!'

'Brian! Tony! Behave yourselves!' Mrs Treadwell is angry and red-faced.

It's not my fault, Brian wants to tell her, but no one ever believes him when he says that. Safety pins! Torn wings! Huh, some angel! As he moves away from Tony, he sees his sister Beth grinning at him and he can't tell if it's in sympathy or malice. Beth is a shepherd with a towel over her head and a stick in her hand. Brian thinks that he would have been a shepherd and Beth an angel except for Mrs Treadwell, who is, as everyone knows, a feminist. She makes boys do girls' things and has girls acting like boys. It's a wonder she hasn't got Christopher Ryan playing Mary.

'Are we ready?' Mrs Treadwell says. 'Matthew, straighten your wings. Alice? Can you hear me, Alice? You're supposed to be next to Beth, and Moana, for goodness' sake, that's baby Jesus, not a cricket bat.'

Amazingly, when the curtains open, everyone is in his or her place and quiet, and the parents are leaning forward with listening faces. André Marchant plays the opening bars of 'Silent Night' and Brian fills his lungs with air. When he opens his mouth a full sound comes out, a whole choir of angels in harmony so beautiful that his back shivers and his eyes prickle and all he can think of is snow – beautiful, white, peaceful snow.

Nothing bad happens. No one forgets their lines, no one's wings fall off and Moana doesn't drop the baby Jesus doll even once. When Beth points to the gold cut-out star at the back of the stage, she smiles at Brian and he smiles back. 'I see a star in the East,' Beth says in a high clear voice, which is the cue for the piano and everyone singing 'While Shepherds Watched Their Flocks by Night' followed by 'O Come All Ye Faithful' with Mrs Treadwell frantically waving a pencil to make them hurry the words. When they come to 'O Little Town of Bethlehem' and the solo verses, Brian looks down into the audience to see three grey veils and three pairs of spectacles reflecting the light, the Sisters of St Joseph the Labourer waiting for his voice. Remembering Sister Agnes's instructions, he breathes deeply from his abdomen and relaxes his jaw to make his mouth a cave full of beautiful sound. The words come out as cleanly as bell notes.

> For Christ is born of Mary,
> And gathered all above,
> While mortals sleep the angels keep
> Their watch of wondering love.
> O morning stars together
> Proclaim the holy birth,
> And praises sing to God the King,
> And peace to us on earth.

Everyone in the audience is watching and the Sisters are smiling, their faces like crumpled paper under the fire of their glasses. Behind them, Liz soundlessly claps her hands. Even Mrs Treadwell, still stabbing the air with her pencil, beams at him and gives a quick nod.

The air is full of miracles.

* * *

That night at the convent, while they are heating the milk for cocoa, Sister Agnes tells him he sang very nicely and then she says, 'Brian, we've sold the convent.'

He doesn't understand. He looks at Sister Mary Clare, who is counting gingernuts onto a plate, and at Sister Luke who stares blindly at the darkened window, smiling and tapping her fingertips together.

'The convent now belongs to Mr Loveridge,' says Sister Agnes, 'but there's no haste. We don't have to vacate until the end of January. Brian, we've been talking to your father and Elizabeth.'

He shakes his head. 'Bishop Chaytor's in Israel. You said after Christmas.' He looks for some sign of teasing, big joke, Brian Collins, got you that time, shot you down in flames, ha ha, but the truth is in Sister Mary Clare's eyes. 'It's too early,' he says, his voice crackling like cellophane.

'We sold it ourselves,' says Sister Agnes. 'That's what's been occupying us this week, but Brian, I've spoken to your father and Elizabeth and they've agreed –'

'No, no!' All he can do is shake his head, for now there are tears thick in his nose and throat and hot in his eyes, and the pain is back, the same terrible pain that fills his breathing and runs down the insides of his arms like hot wires. His shoulders shake as he sobs.

Sister Mary Clare comes to him and holds his head against her. 'Wisha, wisha, you know what I said about miracles.'

He cries against grey cloth, too hurt to remember or speak. He's done everything right, everything, and God's answer has been to hurry up the disaster. What about his mother? Was she wild because he didn't like Liz? Or wild because he tried to be nice to her? What has gone wrong?

Sister Agnes sits in the chair beside him. 'Listen, Brian, there are two things you have to know about miracles. Are you listening? Well, stop that nonsense and sit up straight. Two things. The first is they rarely happen the way we want. Often they turn out better. The second is they don't happen when we're striving for them. It's when we stop, when we let go, that's when God gives us the miracle. Do you understand me?'

No, he doesn't understand and he can't stop crying. Sister Mary Clare pats his head.

Sister Agnes says, 'You'll be living at home with your family. You've always known that. But we've had a word with your Dad and Elizabeth. Brian, will you stop that? Sister Luke, Sister Mary Clare and myself are going on a little holiday and we need our handyman. Your father says you've never been in snow. Is that true?'

The word snow cuts through his grief like a hiccup. He turns away from Sister Mary Clare and wipes his arm across his face, nodding.

Sister Mary Clare says gently, 'So you'll be coming with us. A holiday to the South Island to visit our lovely Patricia, and sure, we'll be finding us snow along the way.'

He sniffs. 'It's summer.'

'Mountains have snow all year round,' says Sister Agnes. 'We'll find enough to build a snowman. Are you interested?'

'Milk, Sisters,' says Sister Luke.

Sister Agnes turns to her. 'We're talking about the snow, Luke. Brian has always wanted to see –'

'Milk, milk!' Sister Luke points with a wavering finger, and immediately there is a hiss on the stove and the strong smell of burning.

'Blessed saints!' Sister Mary Clare grabs the handle and shifts the pot off the ring, while Sister Agnes turns off the element. Puddles of milk bubble, thicken and turn black at the edges. A layer of smoke forms against the ceiling.

The smell fills Brian with new comfort. Burnt milk and snow. 'How will we get there?' he asks, his voice still wet.

'We're buying a car,' says Sister Agnes, reaching for a cloth.

Sister Luke laughs. 'And I'll be driving,' she says.

CHAPTER EIGHT

WHEN THEY TELL BRIAN HE CAN CHOOSE A CAR FOR THEM, he is convinced they are joking, for in spite of the fact that they've lost their home to Mr Loveridge, they've been joking a lot these last two days, teasing with straight faces and then laughing like little kids who get the giggles at the table and can't stop. He has not seen them like this before and the more he thinks about it, the more he is certain there has been a mix-up in prayers. Without doubt a miracle has occurred but it is not his miracle. With all those petitions going up like invisible banners, the inevitable has happened and Brian Collins's mother has received someone else's prayers, which means that some kid in America or Ireland who's asked for a holiday up a mountain is walking through his home town and thinking, hey, that old convent looks like new.

Brian doesn't mind having a holiday. In fact, he's as pleased as anyone could possibly be about eight days in the South Island. He's never been there, never been on a mountain – and snow, oh yes, real snow, he's never actually, not with his feet and hands and breathing in the smell of it, been in snow.

'Nor have I,' says Sister Luke, 'not since I was a little girl in Dublin and there was such a heavy snowfall. The horses pulling the brewery cart. I remember a saddle of snow on their backs and ice like beads threaded on their manes. It was beautiful, Brian. Great is God and greatly to be praised.'

Brian wonders what the mountain snow will be like for Sister Luke now that she is blind. Will it be black instead of white, he asks her.

She turns her head slowly and he notices for the first time how still her eyes are. They move with her head, not by themselves, totally different from Father Friel's eyes, which are the fastest Brian has ever seen, and there is something in them that always looks like a smile. Now the smile reaches down to her mouth as she says, 'My vision is too short, Brian, and the gilt has worn off the gingerbread.'

He goes back to reading the newspaper to her, the boring government bits that she likes best. 'The crises affecting the leadership of the National and Labour Parties have several factors in common including elements of panic and–and polit–i–cal–political imma–t–ur–'

'Immaterial,' she says.

'I don't think so.'

'Immense?'

'Ah – no.'

'It doesn't matter. Go on.'

'The outcome of both dramas has been the only fair one possible – the re–re–tention of Mr Muldoon and Mr Rowling as their parties' respect–re–'

'Respectable.'

'Respect–ful leaders.'

'We have five minutes,' Sister Agnes calls from the kitchen. 'Five minutes and the taxi arrives to take us to the car shop.'

'Taxi?' Sister Luke leans forward. 'Are we spending good money on a taxi?' She waves at Brian. 'Go on.'

He folds the paper. 'The New Zealand Maori Council is the latest to register its oppo–sit–ion to next year's prop–osed

Springbok's rugby tour. The council's positive stand is still further evi–dence of–of–'

'We'll need umbrellas,' says Sister Agnes. 'Yes, definitely umbrellas. Do you realise this rain will be snow on Mount Cook?'

* * *

The rain is not yet heavy. They stand under black umbrellas while it mists down on the Chapman Motors Car Sales yard, which is wet enough to reflect colour in the concrete. The newer cars are at the front, shining paint, window glass freckled with drops of water, the older models sit nearer the back by the office.

'Choose,' says Sister Agnes.

He looks up and realises it isn't a joke. They do expect him to select a car for them. The responsibility fills him with prickling panic. He's a kid, for goodness' sake. What does he know about cars?

'It will need to be roomy for the four of us,' says Sister Agnes, 'a chariot reliable and worthy of our travel.'

'Comfortable seats,' says Sister Luke.

'Luggage space and all,' adds Sister Mary Clare.

He walks away from the umbrellas and feels the feather-touch of rain on his face, his hair. He runs his hand over the bonnet of a Morris van and the drops form trickles beneath his fingers. He can't do this.

They follow, three grey nuns under two black umbrellas, Sister Luke's hand through Sister Mary Clare's arm. 'Take your time,' Sister Agnes calls.

When Brian's father talks about cars, there are words like horsepower and transmission, fuel injection, suspension, radial tyres. Brian knows zero about these things, only that they are important. He walks around a brown Holden station wagon which was new five years ago. It's big and the seats could be comfortable. His hand slides along the doors until his sleeve is soaked to the elbow.

99

Through the rain, he can smell a rich dark brew of oil and tyres and vinyl. He glances at the Sisters, who are smiling as though he has done something very clever.

'Perfect!' says Sister Agnes, clapping her hands together around the stem of her umbrella.

'But the engine mightn't be very good,' he says. 'I don't know about engines and stuff like that.'

'They wouldn't sell a car with an inferior motor,' says Sister Agnes. She tilts her umbrella to the sign over the office. 'There you are, Brian. Read that. Every vehicle guaranteed. I think we can leave the details to the experts.'

'It's being very roomy in the back seat and all,' says Sister Mary Clare, peering through the window. 'You could stretch your legs good and straight and still have space, and there's a little pocket for the maps. Ah Brian, it's grand, so it is.'

But Brian's stomach is spiky with panic. He is remembering, although not in words he can repeat, the things his father has said about car dealers. 'We'd better phone Dad,' he pleads.

They look a question at him.

'The guarantee might be crook,' he says. 'Dad won't mind. He'll look at the engine and tyres and – and transmission and stuff. Nobody'll put anything across you, not with Dad around.'

Their faces smile, tremble, seem on the edge of laughter, then Sister Agnes says, 'Brian, we have the highest guarantees.' She nudges a tyre with her wet black shoe. 'We've prayed about it,' she says.

* * *

Mr Rowe of Chapman Motors wears a pink shirt and a wide tie with music notes on it. He must like music a lot because he keeps talking about the Beatles and how sad it is that John Lennon has been killed, kaput, just like that, a whole world plunged into mourning. The Sisters don't know who John Lennon is but Mr

Rowe doesn't see that in their polite smiles. He likes to talk, does Mr Rowe, and even though the Sisters say they'll take the Holden station wagon, he has to do the sales bit, saying what an amazing model it is, low mileage, only one owner, a real treasure, all this in a tiny office with a girl not much older than Kathy answering the phone, and rain, heavy now, beating against the windows. Brian's hair is wet. Trickles run down his forehead and the back of his neck. He hopes the Sisters can't see the rude calendar on the wall above the batteries.

'How about a test drive?' says Mr Rowe, shaking a key on a tag. 'Wait here, ladies. I'll bring it to the door so you don't get wet.'

That's the third time he's called them ladies. Brian is not sure if it is a compliment or an insult and he is relieved that the Sisters don't seem to notice. He wishes they would let him phone his father. Prayers are not enough, in his opinion, especially after his own prayers have been so mucked up.

The Sisters are watching Mr Rowe run across the yard through pencil lines of rain. He is holding a newspaper over his head but the rain is getting him, scribbling dark blotches on his pink shirt and showing the outline of his singlet.

'Oh Agnes,' says Sister Mary Clare. 'You'll be driving it on the Cook Strait ferry. Will it be too big, do you think?'

'Not at all,' says Sister Agnes. 'They take cattle trucks and trains on the ferry. Look, he's in! The windscreen wipers are going.' She clasps her hands beneath her chin. 'He's driving in reverse and now he's turning.'

Mr Rowe stops the station wagon under the overhang of the office roof, pulls on the handbrake, and gets out. The windscreen wipers squeal on the drying glass. He reaches back through the door, turns off the engine and pulls out the key. 'Now, who's driving?'

'I am,' says Sister Luke, holding out her hand.

He gives her the key and then stands by the door, not noticing their laughter. 'You have to be careful how you put your foot down. She takes off like a space shuttle, nought to sixty from here to the traffic lights.'

'Thank you,' says Sister Luke. She holds the key, her arm stretched and swinging like the needle of a compass. 'Where is the car?' she asks in the same polite voice.

He looks at her, looks again, and realises that she is blind. His words stop. His mouth remains open.

Sister Agnes takes the keys from Sister Luke. 'I'm sorry,' she says. 'It was our little joke. I'm the driver. I have a motor car licence.'

He closes his mouth but forgets to put it back in its smile, and Sister Agnes gets in, tucking her habit around her. Sister Mary Clare opens the back door. Brian holds it while she helps Sister Luke in behind the driver's seat. Then she and Brian walk around the back and get in on the other side. Brian breathes deeply. The smell is thrilling, polish, vinyl, black rubber mats, nearly newness.

'Very comfortable seats,' says Sister Mary Clare, bouncing a little.

'Praise God,' murmurs Sister Luke. 'Praise be He from whom all blessings flow.'

Sister Agnes fits the key in the ignition. Mr Rowe still holds her door. Sister Agnes says to him, 'Are we ready?'

He jumps like someone waking from a sleep and his smile comes back. 'Wherever you like. Around the block. Out on the highway. Give it a good run and you'll see for yourselves, she's absolutely faultless.'

'You'll be coming too,' says Sister Agnes.

Mr Rowe's smile gets bigger as he spreads his hands. 'If I can't trust you ladies, then who can I trust?'

'But we need you,' says Sister Agnes. 'You have to show me where the gears are.'

* * *

Brian's father was wrong when he said Sister Agnes was a terrible driver. Brian discovers she's a perfectly good driver, once she's worked out the gears, and they have no problems going through town, stopping at traffic lights, turning corners. In fact, she drives as well as Brian's Dad, only slower.

Mr Rowe thinks she's too slow. 'You can go more than 40 ks on the open road,' he says in a ha-ha voice.

'Not when it's raining,' says Sister Agnes. 'I believe in being careful.'

Sister Luke laughs. 'It's raining, it's pouring, the old man is snoring.'

'Think on it,' says Sister Mary Clare, 'all this rain turning to big fluffy snowflakes on the mountains. Mr Rowe, would you be telling us, does this car go up steep mountain roads?'

Mr Rowe has been tapping his fingers on the side window. He tries to turn his head to the back seat. 'Steep mountains, steep walls, you can take her anywhere, ladies. Will she let you down? No way, José. This is one honey of a wagon. It's eating my heart out I can't keep her for myself.' His fingers resume tapping. 'The services for John Lennon, did you see them on tele? Millions of people all over the world. The Archbishop of Canterbury, now he was born in Liverpool, same as the Beatles. Did you see him?'

'Dr Robert Runcie,' says Sister Luke.

Mr Rowe says, 'Is he one of your lot?'

'A cousin,' says Sister Agnes, who is holding the top of the steering wheel with both hands, and leaning forward to peer through the beating windscreen wipers.

Mr Rowe swings back. 'No kidding? The Archbishop of Canterbury your cousin?'

'A cousin in the faith,' says Sister Agnes.

Mr Rowe doesn't speak again until a car that's been following them beeps loudly, dah, dah, dah, then he says to Sister Agnes, 'You can go a bit faster and still be safe.'

'Not in the rain,' she says.

Brian rests his head against the cool glass. His clothes have dried and he has the pleasure of looking at rain from a comfortable place. They're in the country now, wet sheep in wet grass, water gleaming on every shed and fence post. The wipers thud gentle little beats to the tune of hissing tyres.

'What colour is our new vehicle?' asks Sister Luke.

'Brown,' says Brian.

Mr Rowe corrects him. 'It's called mushroom.'

'Light fawn, Luke dear,' says Sister Mary Clare.

Dah, dah, dah, goes the car behind.

'They want to get past,' says Mr Rowe.

'With this traffic and these conditions, passing would be very dangerous,' says Sister Agnes.

Dah, dah, da-a-a-a-ah! The car with the blaring horn, a red Mazda, sweeps alongside and cuts across in front of them, almost hitting an oncoming truck.

'Well!' says Sister Agnes. 'Did you see that!'

'I have been to Canterbury Cathedral,' says Sister Luke. 'It was very impressive. Henry the Eighth had six wives.'

The Mazda races away, fire engine red, into the rain.

'Such carelessness!' says Sister Luke. 'Thank God they didn't hit that truck – or us. That's another reason why we need a big car, Mr Rowe. It gives us a greater degree of safety on the highway.'

Mr Rowe doesn't answer and Brian thinks that the salesman has finally used up all his words.

'Colour is important,' says Sister Luke, 'even when you're blind.'

* * *

With so much stuff in the garage, the station wagon must be parked on the road and they have to run through the pelting rain, umbrellas up, Sister Luke holding onto Sister Mary Clare's arm, through the little gate, along the path to the steps, quick, Brian, quick, get the key, and into the porch where umbrellas and grey skirts are shaken like wet dogs and Sister Luke leans against the doorway, hand at her throat, saying, 'My heart, oh dear God!' Sister Mary Clare gives her a tablet to put under her tongue and sits her down on a kitchen chair, telling her that the excitement has been enough to unravel the knitting of anybody's heart and there, Sister dear, it'll be a fine cup of tea coming up.

An hour later the rain has stopped, Sister Luke rests upstairs with Sister Mary Clare looking after her, and Sister Agnes gives Brian a bowl to pick strawberries before they get spoiled with all the wetness. She follows with another bowl to get runner beans for the evening meal, her gumboots squelching in the grass and her habit wetting to a darker grey around the hem.

Usually it is Sister Mary Clare who is with him in the garden. With Sister Agnes he is more careful about the way he does things on account of her eyes sharp for mistakes. It came, his father told him, from all those years of marking exam papers. He opens the garden gate for her and she limps in, squishing mud. All the vegetables are heavy with water, silverbeet leaves turned down like the pages of books, cabbages weighted with huge glassy drops. She goes to the bean trellis where green leaves, red flowers and new little beans glisten with wetness. She says, 'Nine bean rows will I have there, a hive for the honey bees. "Lake Isle of Innisfree", Brian. Do you know it?'

'Yes, Sister. William Butler Yeats.'

She looks surprised. 'Oh? They're teaching Yeats in Standard Three?'

'No, Sister. It was you, Sister.'

'If you want to know more about God, Brian, read poetry. Yeats, Gerard Manley Hopkins, Wordsworth.' She smiles. 'I told you that last week, didn't I?'

'Yes, Sister.'

'And I read "Innisfree" to you last week.'

'Yes, Sister.'

'It was kind of you not to remind me that I'm losing my marbles. Stand back.' With the palm of her hand, she hits the end of the bean frame so that it shivers and drops a waterfall to the earth. 'No need to get any wetter than necessary,' she says, and begins to pick beans.

Brian lifts the wire mesh from the strawberries and bends over, touching wet leaves, looking for the colour red amongst white flowers and unripe fruit. Drops of water slide away from his touch and flower petals stick to his fingers. He carefully picks a bright red fruit and wipes dirt off it against his shirt. He glances up, sees Sister Agnes's back, and puts the strawberry in his mouth. Runner beans and strawberries are like poetry, he thinks. He doesn't know why. They just are.

Sister Agnes says, 'This used to be a very big garden, you know, extending halfway across the lawn. We grew vegetables for ourselves and families in the parish – onions, carrots, pumpkins. When your father was not much older than you, he helped me dig potatoes. Oh, he did, and he used to smell them. He'd lift a potato from the earth and hold it under his nose. "Sister," he'd say, "you can't beat the smell of a potato fresh out of the ground." I wonder if he remembers that.' She shakes her head. 'We were a thriving community in those days. If anyone had told us we were an endangered species, we'd have considered them quite ridiculous.'

He understands about the potatoes. He has his father's nose.

'The last of the dinosaurs,' she says, snapping a bean off the vine.

'When we come back from holiday,' he says, 'what will happen?'

'You'll go home,' she says.

He finds another strawberry. 'I know, but Sister Mary Clare said I can help pack things.'

'I don't think so, Brian. There'll be Christmas to keep you occupied and then I think your father plans to take all the family to the beach for most of January.'

'We always go to the beach.'

'After that, you'll be getting ready for school again. There are people in the parish who can help with the packing.'

His throat hurts and he tries not to cry. 'I don't have to go with them to the silly old beach.'

'I think you do,' she says firmly. 'You can always visit us when you get back.'

He wipes his hand across his eyes. 'I can't go all the way to Wellington,' he says, and his voice comes out angry.

Sister Agnes turns to him with the bowl of beans held against her apron. 'Brian, didn't we tell you? We're not going to the Sisters of

Mercy. We're not moving to Wellington. We are buying a house in this parish.'

'Here?'

'Maybe even in your street. Who knows but God? We'll start looking as soon as we get back from the South Island. I imagine we'll have it by Christmas. A tidy four-bedroomed house, reasonably new, no maintenance. Imagine it, Brian. No leaking roof or broken window frames, no sagging foundations. We don't anticipate much lawn or garden but I'm sure we'd appreciate your ongoing assistance when you have time to spare.'

'Really?' The surprise of it comes up in him like a bubble of laughter. 'You're actually getting a new convent!'

'Not exactly. More of a retirement –' She smiles. 'You've been praying for the old convent to be renewed.'

He nods. 'Yes, yes! It's Mum! You know, she's my patron saint. And I thought, Sister, I thought –'

'I suppose the house will be a new convent,' she says, 'and we can definitely call it a miracle. We owe it to your prayers, Brian. Make sure you thank God and your dear mother.'

'I will, Sister! You bet I will. I thought when it didn't happen, I thought the prayers got mixed up. I didn't know. I –' He finds another strawberry. 'There was something else, too, Sister. I asked for you to get better, your bones and Sister Mary Clare's asthma and Sister Luke –'

'Why, Brian?'

He doesn't answer immediately. His mind is suddenly filled with a picture of his mother in hospital, face thin, eyes big and bright as fire. He blinks the image away. 'Because – because I didn't want you to be sick.'

'Come here, Brian.' Sister Agnes beckons with her finger.

He puts down his strawberry bowl, stands, and walks to her, tucking in his shirt.

She says, 'I'm not a storyteller like Sister Mary Clare but listen, do you know what a parable is?'

He nods.

'This isn't a parable you'll find in Scripture. Some are, some aren't. Suppose you have a beautiful home where you are free and very, very happy, and something happens. You are taken away and put in prison. It's a small prison with thick walls so you can't escape. But for most of the time, it's not an uncomfortable prison. People look after you. They give you food. After a while you get used to it and you forget about your beautiful home. But in the prison, there is a tiny window high in the wall for those who can see. When you look out of it, you get a glimpse of home and your heart feels faint with longing. Oh, you so want to be there! You find yourself spending more and more time at the window, as the years go by. Then one day you see a crack in the wall of the prison. A little while later, another crack. The wall is starting to crumble. Your prison is breaking down. Are you listening, Brian?'

'Yes, Sister.'

'How would you feel if some workmen came along and said, "We're here to repair your prison. We'll make it as good as new." '

He shrugs and leans sideways to scratch the back of his knee.

'How would you feel, Brian?'

'I don't know, Sister. I – I never thought the old convent was like a prison. Honest. It's beautiful. It's like – really like home.' He scratches again.

'No, no! I'm not talking about the convent. I'm talking about us. People. Human beings. That's the parable, Brian. Your real self is your soul which comes from God. The prison is your body.'

'Oh.'

'When the prison breaks down we go home to God where we belong. Do you understand?'

Yes, he thinks he does. Well, most of it. His mother, the white face, the eyes. He thinks he understands but when he tries to hold the knowledge, it slides away from words. 'Yes, Sister. But why do we go to prison, Sister?'

'That is a mystery resting with God. But I am sure the mystery is to do with growth. This is where our souls grow. That's what life's all about.'

'Yes, Sister.'

'I'm sure you have a knowing, Brian. You've got the gift. In your heart you know that little window and there is a restlessness in you that draws you to it. Prayer, Brian. The window is prayer. That's where you see home.'

'Yes, Sister.'

'But don't pray for my bones, there's a good lad.'

'No, Sister.'

'You can do better things with prayers. Where did you put your bowl? Bless my soul, boy, is that all? Or have you been eating strawberries behind my back?'

***

On Sunday morning Sister Agnes drives to Mass, leaving early so that they can park the station wagon directly outside the church. Father Friel sees them and comes running down the steps, smiling and wiping his hands together. He pulls open Sister Luke's door. 'You've got it!'

'A brown motor car to take us to Patricia,' says Sister Luke, accepting his assistance. 'God is good and so is the bank.'

Father Friel laughs. 'Not bad at all. What year – 75? 76? It'll do you. Run for years, this model. A bit on the big side. Are you managing it all right, Agnes? Good, good. You'll be needing a decent-size garage, I reckon.'

So he knows, thinks Brian. Father Friel knows they are going to buy a new convent.

'After the holidays,' says Sister Mary Clare, getting out the other door. 'We've looked in the papers and sure now there are houses for the picking. Just as long as it's close to the shops and church.'

'Before the bishop gets back,' says Sister Luke.

Father Friel thrusts his big hands up in the air. 'Don't tell me! I know nothing!' he says, the bigness of him shaking with laughter.

That stops when he sees Brian. 'Why aren't you home where you belong?' he says.

'He'll be home before Christmas,' says Sister Agnes, scooping herself out of the driver's seat. 'He's going with us to the South Island.' She looks at Father Friel and before he can open his mouth, says, 'We need his help.'

They go up the steps, Sister Luke holding Father Friel's arm, and Brian sees that the church pews are empty. This is about the earliest they've ever been. He says to Father Friel, 'Can I have reconciliation, Father?'

'Now?'

'I couldn't come yesterday,' he says. 'I was helping to buy the Holden station wagon.'

'All right, all right. Hurry up.'

They go into the new confessional with the two chairs, and Father Friel kisses his stole, puts it around his neck, sighs. He has food marks on the black jersey Sister Mary Clare mended for him.

'Well, don't just sit there, Brian.'

'Bless me, Father, I have sinned. It's been a week since my last confession.'

'As long as that?'

'Yes, Father. Father, I confess the sin of pride, the sin of doubt, the sin of anger, and I am deeply sorry –'

'Brian, will you forget the nuns' talk and tell me what this is about?'

He hesitates. The interruption has caused him to lose his place. 'It was about this miracle, Father. I was praying and I thought it didn't happen and I got really mad with God but actually it did happen, only different.'

'Brian?'

'Yes, Father?'

'Get out of here.'

* * *

'It doesn't matter what they said. You should have phoned me.'
Brian's father has a toaster apart on the kitchen table. He's putting
in a new bi-metallic strip, bits of metal together, one stretching more
than the other with heat, so that the strip bends and the toast pops
up. It looks very complicated to Brian, who has become accustomed
to the Sisters' toaster. 'They were diddled,' his Dad adds.

Brian, who has been expecting praise, says defensively, 'Father
Friel thinks it's a good car.'

'The car's all right,' Dad says. 'It's not the car. It's the money
they paid, a good eight hundred more than it's worth. I should have
been there.' He fits a small screwdriver on the head of a screw. 'Nuns
are hopeless with money.'

Brian watches until the screw is in place, then he says, 'Sister
Agnes isn't a terrible driver. She's really careful.'

'Yeah, yeah. Twenty miles an hour.'

'No.'

'Twenty miles an hour hanging onto the wheel as though it's
going to fall off. Don't tell me no, I've seen it.'

Brian shakes his head. 'It wasn't. She went forty ks.'

'Same difference.'

'She drives really good. Good as anything, Dad.'

'There'll be an accident, mark my words.' Dad points the
screwdriver at him. 'Do up your seat-belt, son. The only consideration is at that speed, it's not likely to be a serious accident. Bicycle
running up the exhaust pipe.' Dad laughs at his own joke, then
blows some crumbs out of the toaster. 'You won't get on the ferry
tomorrow.'

'Yes we will. Sister Agnes says it's easy.'

'I'm not talking about the driving, you daft beggar. The ticket.
They won't get a booking for the car.'

'They will. They've prayed about it.'

His father gives him a long look and takes the pliers out of his
tool kit. 'Prayer is prayer. Okay. Now here, Brian, are the facts of
life.' He places the pliers on the table, the screwdriver near it. 'This
is the North Island. This is the South Island. Between is Cook Strait,

ten miles of rolling ocean. School has finished. Holidays have started. The traffic in the South Island is going north for Christmas and the traffic from the north is going south. The ferries have been booked up for months, and there are long, long waiting lists. Got it?'

Brian stares at the pliers and screwdriver and says nothing.

'Son, I'm telling you this so you won't be disappointed.' Dad puts his hand on Brian's arm. 'Even if you did get down there, you wouldn't see snow at this time of year.'

'Mountains,' says Brian.

'Right,' says Dad, 'from a distance.'

'Sister Mary Clare asked Mr Rowe and he said the Holden would go up steep mountain roads no trouble at all.'

'Who's Mr –? Oh. Salesman. He'd tell you it'd go to the moon. Brian, there are no roads. This time of year there's no way to get to snow without climbing steep rock faces so you'd better get that into your head. Look, I know how you get set on things. Next winter we'll go to Mount Ruapehu, and this time I'm making it a solemn promise, cross my heart and hope to die. All right, peanut face?'

Brian nods as Liz comes into the kitchen, holding Joey's hand.

'I can make you those new curtains,' Liz says.

* * *

Brian thinks that nuns' news like nuns' prayers might have instant effect, but while the prayers go up to heaven, the news whisks through the parish like the equinoctial nor'wester, blowing in people's ears and out again through their mouths. Take Uncle Barry and Aunty Joan, for instance, no sooner do they open the front door than they start on at Dad, asking if it is true.

'It's their convent,' says Dad. 'They can do what they like with it. Brian, go and play outside, there's a good lad.'

Brian goes into the hall and stands against the darkest part of the wall by the old family pictures. He looks at his father, twelve years old, at the beach with Grandpa Collins, an old man with Sister Agnes's face. If Mr Liam Collins had been a girl, he and Sister Agnes could have been identical twins.

'Oh! Just imagine when the bishop comes back!' cries Aunty Joan, and then she laughs, more like a shriek.

'That'll be when the shite'll hit the fan,' says Uncle Barry.

'Why should it?' says Dad. 'I'm sure he's been counting on it, but it wasn't his to sell. It was their decision. They said when it came down to it, they couldn't move out of the parish. Look at their work here. Nearly three generations of families. But do you know what they did? They undercut Bill Chaytor's price. They went to Loveridge and said he could have it for government valuation, no more, no less, because that was – now get this – that was justice.'

'No-o-o-o!' says Aunty Joan.

'Matthew Loveridge is worth millions!' roars Uncle Barry.

'Dropped to two forty,' says Dad, and Brian hears groaning laughter.

'What are they doing? Getting a new convent?' Uncle Barry asks.

'Yep. That's why we can't go to the beach before Christmas,' says Dad. 'I told them I'd help them buy a house. Check it out for them, make sure they get what they pay for. You know they went ahead with a car – wait a minute.' He raises his voice, 'Brian! If you're standing by the door, go out and play this minute!'

* * *

The sunset looks like melted butter over everything, lawn, garden, gate, car, even the old rusty wheelbarrow is gold-washed. Brian has oiled the barrow wheel and pumped up its tyre so that it trundles between the convent and the station wagon without complaint, bearing, over several trips, the bags, the rugs, Sister Luke's pillow, the chilly bin. They must pack the car tonight because they are leaving at dawn for Wellington and the Cook Strait ferry.

Brian is filled with a pleasure so fierce, he thinks he may not sleep at all. He wants to phone his father and say that twenty-three years ago Sister Agnes gave a sack of potatoes and a fruit cake to the mother of a man in the ferry ticket office, so there, but he doesn't because that might be the sin of pride and he's bargaining for another miracle, a snowfall on almost the longest day of the year.

As the sun sets over the sea, Sister Mary Clare helps him stow the last of the bags and lock the wagon. Her wide face, normally the colour of pink marshmallow, is covered with the golden light that she calls happiness paint. 'Sure now, Brian, back home this is the time when the little folk are everywhere, just everywhere, gathering happiness paint in the tiniest pottles. On sad winter days they'll pour it down chimneys, a special blessing for good children, so they will. The colour of the dying sun. It's very powerful, Brian.'

'Like the blood of the cross?' he asks.

She puts her head on one side. 'Well now, I never in my life thought of that, Brian, which goes to show you're a very deep thinker. It's a sign of the vocation, you know.'

He shrugs.

'How does Father Brian Collins sound to you?' She smiles, half teasing.

'Like hard work, Sister,' he says, teasing back.

She laughs and waves her hands. 'Oh, get away with you and your wheelbarrow. But don't put it in the shed. There's one more thing to come down in the morning.'

'One more?'

'The Ark of the Covenant,' she says.

* * *

She means Mother Magdala's chest. It has been polished so that the carving on the lid stands out something beautiful, twisting lines of Celtic knots and the Irish words meaning 'Work with Reverence', which is the motto of the Sisters of St Joseph the Labourer. Reverence in all endeavours, Sister Agnes says, whether it be washing dishes or cleaning a floor, for when you do something with reverence, you'll find God in it, even a simple thing like eating a boiled egg.

Brian doesn't know how God on his throne can get into a boiled egg but he guesses that it's something to do with the Holy Spirit, which is everywhere, and he wonders if that includes chewing gum, which Sister Agnes detests. There are so many things he doesn't know. He would have to learn a terrible lot if he was going to be a priest. An electrician might be easier.

Working with reverence means being slow and quiet and very neat. They put Mother Magdala's chest on the altar and place a white cloth inside it. They bless themselves and then wrap their silver tabernacle in another white cloth, and put it in the chest.

Sister Agnes says, 'Lord be with us in our leaving.'

Sister Mary Clare says, 'Lord be with us in our journey.'

They look to Sister Luke, who has one hand on the corner of the altar. 'Lord be with us in a safe return,' she says. 'Amen, amen.'

Now Sister Mary Clare spreads another white cloth and starts to wrap one of the silver candlesticks. Without a word, Sister Agnes puts out her long bony fingers, the too-big gold ring wound with cotton, and lays them on top of Sister Mary Clare's plump pink hand. The Sisters look at each other in a moment of stillness. Then Sister Mary Clare puts the silver candlestick back on the altar and reaches for Brian's Advent candle in its pine cone wreath. She wraps it very slowly and puts it in the chest with the tabernacle. They close the lid and genuflect.

They carry the chest to the back door and Brian watches as Sister Mary Clare spreads a rug over the wheelbarrow. She arranges it just so, with three corners hanging not quite to the ground, and the fourth, above the wheel, tucked over.

'Is it all right to put the Blessed Sacrament in a rusty old wheelbarrow?' he asks, not quite believing it.

'Of course,' she says. 'Would you be knowing how many years this good barrow has worked for Himself. Like a donkey and not even asking grass to eat. Our Lord loves this wheelbarrow, Brian, and to be sure he'll be glad to honour it.'

There is a procession down the path saying morning prayers, with Sister Mary Clare pushing the chest in the barrow, Sister Agnes walking in front and Sister Luke behind with her hands on Brian's shoulder, blessed be the Lord, the God of Israel, he has visited his people and redeemed them, the sky pale between night and day, and the air cool, smelling of wet grass and lavender, down to the gate and then the car, singing, singing, he has raised up for us a mighty saviour in the house of David his servant, as he promised by the lips of the holy, those who were his prophets of old.

Brian has his own prayer, one word with every deliberate foot-fall, snow, snow, snow, snow, snow, snow, snow.

CHAPTER NINE

W HEN THE FERRY ENTERS THE SOUNDS, THEY GO OUT ON deck and sit in a bright breeze which flutters the Sisters' veils and makes an arc of the wool from Sister Mary Clare's knitting. Sister Luke, next to Brian, wants to know what they're passing and he describes it all, working systematically from sky to sea to boat so he doesn't miss anything.

'The seagulls aren't really flying, just riding on air. White with red beaks and red feet folded up. Hardly any clouds, Sister. Smudgy bits, kind of like toothpaste on a mirror. The hills are farms, I think, grass and some trees and sheep and a white house with a wharf going into the sea. It's not a beach. Just rocks, Sister. There's seaweed, brown patches floating up to the top of the water.'

'What colour is the water?'

'Green, Sister. Green by the shore and kind of bluey in the middle. There's a boat coming up. That's white too. I think they're fishing. There's something – a fish! A fish!'

'What sort of fish?'

'I don't know. There are more. Heaps more! They're huge!'

'Look, Agnes!' Sister Mary Clare drops her knitting.

Sister Agnes stands, clasps her hands under her chin. 'Oh Luke! We're in a school of dolphins.'

'Dolphins!' Brian shouts, jumping up and down. 'Sister, they're dolphins.'

Sister Luke smiles in the opposite direction. 'Great is God and greatly to be praised!' she says. 'Cast your net in deep waters, Brian. Dolphins are lucky. You realise that, don't you? Father Friel's horse won by a nose.'

* * *

It looks as though it has fallen down the hills and come to rest against the sea, Picton, a small town, white buildings with green hills behind and water in front and boats dotted all over the harbour. Brian's parents had their honeymoon in Picton. There are photos of Brian's mother in a sunfrock catching a cod, his father riding a motor scooter. Brian thinks that although his mother has gone to heaven, her footprints will still be in the Picton streets and his sandshoes will touch them like feet kissing feet. He laughs, feeling the rightness of everything as Sister Agnes drives the station wagon slowly, bump, bump, over the ferry ramp and onto the road, Mum with Jesus in heaven, Brian with Jesus in the car, the honeymoon place, a different island like another country, a journey south to snow, it all comes together like voices in a choir, to say one thing. He doesn't know what that one thing is. It's just there. He holds the seat-belt in both hands and pulls it out and in like elastic. It's too much to sit still.

'We're going to Picton town,' he tells Sister Luke.

Sister Agnes parks near the shops and they walk across the road to a café where they order three cups of tea and one milkshake. Brian kicks his legs, tock, tock, against the table leg and Sister Agnes doesn't say a word. They're feeling it too, like Christmas, the happiness paint down the chimney, miracles everywhere bubbling away like lemonade and making them smile.

The tea is a long time coming. 'I'm sorry,' says the woman with the tray. 'I've been busy.'

'That's all right, dear,' says Sister Agnes. 'They also serve who only stand and wait. That's Milton. Do you know Milton?'

The woman shakes her head.

'We're being on holiday and in no hurry at all,' says Sister Mary Clare.

* * *

Back on the pavement, Brian stamps his feet to leave another set of Collins footprints in Picton, stamp, stamp, across the road to the car, but it's hard to walk heavy when you're floating with lightness like some little leaf. He holds out his arms and waggles his fingers. If he were a seagull he could ride the wind to the mountains, to the South Pole, around the world and back again.

'Don't slam the door,' warns Sister Luke. 'We travel with the Lord.'

Sister Agnes unfolds a map on the steering wheel. 'We'll go as far as Kaikoura tonight, God willing. There used to be a convent at Kaikoura but I believe that, too, has been sold. We'll find a motel.'

'How long till we get there, Sister?' Brian asks.

'I'm not sure. Three hours or more. Do you need a restroom, Brian?'

'No, Sister. I went on the ferry.'

'Very well, then.' Sister Agnes folds the map. 'Light-hearted we take to the open road.'

Sister Mary Clare turns in her seat to look at Brian and Sister Luke. 'Have you got room back there? Oh, but it's a lovely car, isn't it? Just the grandest car for a holiday, us all in and not a care in God's beautiful world. Did you take your heart pill, Sister, dear? Fine, fine. Brian, are you comfortable? I'm after thinking this time tomorrow we'll be approaching near the doorstep of our lovely Patricia. Can you see the face of her when we drive up in the new car? God forgive the vanity of me. And our Brian with us? Agnes, is this my seat-belt or yours? I think it's yours, dear. Should we be switching on a little cool air?'

Sister Agnes drives them through Picton town and out into the country. For a while, Brian tells Sister Luke about the farms they pass, but it all looks much the same and Sister Luke doesn't appear to be listening. He closes his eyes, imagining that he too is blind and that his sight will miraculously be restored the instant they come to something interesting, but the darkness inside his eyelids takes him to some deep, far-away place, and the next thing he knows, he is lying against Sister Luke, cheek pressed to rough grey cloth, the click click of her rosary beads close to his ear. He sits up and looks at her, ready to say something, but she is in her prayers, lips moving, no sound coming out but the s's, a faint hissing like a hole in a balloon. He sits up further. Sister Agnes and Sister Mary Clare are talking in the front, and out of the side window there is water, a great calm sea that goes so far it smudges itself into the sky.

'Beaches!' he says.

'That was a long nap,' says Sister Agnes.

'Bless you,' says Sister Mary Clare. 'You were snoring like a pig with its nose stuck in the trough.'

'No, he wasn't,' says Sister Agnes. 'He didn't make a sound. We're getting near Kaikoura, Brian. We should be there by five o'clock.'

'Can we stop at a beach, Sister?' he asks. 'There are heaps of them and nobody there.'

'A beach?' Sister Agnes keeps driving. 'You mean one of these bays? I really don't know. Sisters, should we stop for a breath of fresh salt air?'

Sister Luke folds her beads between her hands. 'Are we by the sea?'

'Lovely sea,' says Sister Mary Clare. 'Flat as a breadboard, no waves at all, and sand the colour of our cloth. Little rocks out there with seaweed lying on the water. Now what would those little red balls be?'

Brian sits tall and stretches his neck. 'They're buoys, Sister. You know, floats. Fishermen have them on nets and crayfish catchers.'

'Lobster pots?' says Sister Luke. 'How nice. I don't fancy sardines in tomato sauce. They always taste tinny. Yes, I think I would like to be on a beach.'

'Can we stop?' he asks.

'Indeed we can, as soon as we can find a parking place,' says Sister Agnes.

A little further on, there is a flat gravelled area off the road and Sister Agnes turns the station wagon into it. At once a line of cars speeds past, about a dozen of them going flat out like a train, and Brian thinks that maybe Sister Agnes does go a bit on the slow side. But she is very careful. Driving with reverence, he thinks. That's it. That's what she's doing. Driving careful with the Blessed Sacrament in the car.

The instant they stop, he has his door open and is out. The air wraps around him with delicious smells of salt and rotting seaweed, a glorious stink of it that has him running through spiky grass and shingle and down onto the beach. He slides in sand, kicking it, crunching it, spraying it up behind him, and when his shoes are full, he sits down to take them off. It's a warm sand and it has in it sharp surprises of shell and dried seaweed pods. He runs, hops, gets to the water's edge and jumps. Oh, the water's cold, wonderfully cold around his ankles.

'Brian?' calls Sister Mary Clare. 'Don't be going in too far, now.'

Nothing is happening to that entire big sea. It is sound asleep, breathing up and down, up and down, no waves, just a small shelf of foam that sighs around his feet. He listens and laughs. The sea is snoring. Yes, like a pig with its nose stuck in a trough, grating pebbles with each breath. Can the Sisters hear it? He looks back and sees them sitting together on the bank above the line of seaweed and driftwood. Two of them are taking off their sandals and socks.

When they come down to the water, he realises that people's feet are a lot like their hands. Sister Mary Clare's are round and pink with toes that turn up like her fingers. Sister Agnes has long bony feet with knobs and blue veins. He looks down at his own, brown, short, spattered with freckles, one toenail black and just about falling off. The sea washes over them, snore, snore, like a pig. Laughing, he kicks water so high that it comes down on his head and shirt.

The Sisters look his way and smile. They are walking one behind the other, at the join of beach and water, their hands behind their backs, their feet barely disturbing the edge of the sea. Their lips move but he doesn't know if they're talking or praying. He looks back up the beach at Sister Luke, who is sitting quite still on the bank, and the knowledge of her blindness suddenly fills him. He walks up the beach, bent over and searching, finding a flat white shell, a piece of glass smoothed to a frosty green, a brown kelp pod. There is more further on, a bit of driftwood shaped like a small dragon, a seagull's feather, another shell with a hole in the middle.

'Sister?' He sits beside her. 'Hold out your hands.'

She doesn't say anything. She examines the collection, one piece at a time, very slowly, her fingers touching each part of the wood, the glass, the shells. She puts the feather to her cheek and traces it around her face as though she is drawing patterns on her skin, then she puts the seaweed pod under her nose and smells it. When she has finished, she does it all over again, wood, glass, shells, feather, seaweed, in the same order, smiling to herself. He watches her but doesn't speak because that might interrupt something. The sea is light with late afternoon sun. Happiness paint, he thinks. Millions of gallons of happiness paint. The hills on the other side of the road are in deep shadow and behind them are mountains, steep grey rock with not a trace of snow. But there will be snow further south where the mountains are closer to Antarctica. Yes, there will be snow. Sister Agnes has said it.

After a while, the others come back, Sister Mary Clare carrying his socks and shoes. 'The fishes didn't want them,' she says.

'We need to be on the road,' says Sister Agnes.

Sister Luke stands up. The beach treasures fall to the ground, all but the piece of glass, which she puts in her pocket where she keeps her beads. 'The world is too much with us,' she says.

* * *

When the woman in the motel asks Sister Agnes for a cheque in advance, Sister Agnes tells her she can pay with cash. She opens her black handbag and Brian gasps, for in it is more money than he has ever seen, a wedge of notes like a great fat book. The motel woman also looks surprised. As they leave the office, Sister Agnes says the woman probably thinks they've robbed a bank.

'Thieves do that, you know,' she tells Brian. 'They dress as priests and religious sisters to avoid suspicion. It has caused extraordinary problems for real clergy and religious, who are always being searched by customs officers.' She looks at the numbers on the key tags. 'They don't have any four-bedroom units but we have two with two bedrooms and they should be next to each other.'

The motel is opposite the beach and is old, smelling so strongly of salt and damp anyone would think the sea came over it every night. Brian bounces on his bed, which has squeaky wire mesh like his bed at the convent, and wonders if he will be left in this unit by himself. But it's all right. Sister Mary Clare and Sister Luke will be in the next room, their heads near the wall to hear if anything happens to him. Sister Agnes is in the next unit and her other bedroom is to be the prayer room.

Sister Mary Clare says, 'Did you notice both of these motel units have a television?'

'One for you and one for me,' says Sister Luke.

Brian looks at her quickly, then realises it is another joke, like offering to drive the car. He thinks perhaps Sister Luke's blindness is the reason why they don't have TV at the convent.

'The car, the car, now,' Sister Agnes reminds them. 'As soon as we've unpacked it, we can give some consideration to the evening meal. Luke, you rest here. It won't be long before you have your tea.'

'Fish and chips would be rather nice,' says Sister Luke.

'Maybe we'll just watch the news,' Sister Mary Clare says, looking at the buttons below the television screen.

* * *

When they've brought in the bags, the Sisters go back for Mother Magdala's chest. One of them could have carried the box easily, but they both do it, holding it up high between them and walking slowly, their footsteps matching. Brian wonders if the motel woman is watching.

In the same slow and deliberate way they bring it into Sister Agnes's unit, take it to the back bedroom and open it. They set a white cloth and the tabernacle on the chest of drawers in the corner. The candle is placed nearby. They take a step backwards and bow low, Sister Mary Clare colliding with one of the two beds that take up most of the space in the room. Brian watches. He is not sure about the motel being a suitable place for the Blessed Sacrament. He looks at the pale yellow walls, the water-stained ceiling, curtains patterned with cartoon crabs and starfish and he is glad that at least they have his Advent candle to make the room a bit holy.

'Close the door, Brian,' says Sister Agnes in her schoolteacher voice. 'You can come with me to get the fish and chips.'

* * *

That night, curled in the hollow of the motel bed with the sound of the sea in the distance, he has a wonderful dream of his mother. She is very beautiful but she doesn't look like an angel. She is wearing a blue dress with red high heels and red earrings that hang down amongst her black hair and she is dancing towards him, holding out her hands, smiling. He can see the shining of her eyes, her lipstick, the red stones in the earrings that fall forward when she bends over to kiss him. Her breath, her touch are warm and her perfume is like all the flowers he has ever smelled.

'I thought you were dead!' he cries.

She laughs at that, puts her hands on her hips, her head back, laughs as though he has made a very funny joke. 'Oh Brian,' she says, 'there's no such thing as dead.'

CHAPTER TEN

WHILE THE SISTERS ARE HAVING MORNING PRAYER, BRIAN takes his dream to the beach where he runs with it up and down the sand, jumping the colours of her dress and shoes, spinning the warmth of her face, laughing her laugh to the pale pink air and the seagulls who watch from a distance. For Brian, dreams are compulsory films and most of them are frightening, dreams of being chased, killed, eaten. Good dreams are rare and he hasn't had a dream about his mother since her funeral, when he saw her as a candle, tall, slender, carved from white wax and burning down until there was nothing but flame, and he woke from that dream crying out with fear. Last night was different, so real that her voice, the smell and touch are still contained inside him and if he fills his lungs with this cool salty air, memory changes it to a garden of flowers. Even her earrings, he sees the winking redness of them in the cloud that rests on the face of the rising sun, a parked car, the collar of a dog being walked on the beach. Every spot of red changes before his eyes to red stones swinging in gold and red shoes with heels as thin as pencils. Oh Brian. Each movement of air is her breath. Oh Brian, oh Brian. He practises long jumps in the sand, leaping from mark to mark until his legs turn to rubber, then he finds a piece of driftwood like a baseball bat and hits shells out to sea until his arms also get tired. Still she comes towards him, the folds in her blue dress swinging. Oh Brian.

* * *

At breakfast he tells the Sisters about his dream and Sister Luke says it is a sign. 'Dreams are letters from God,' she tells him.

He looks into his cornflakes, remembering a roaring lion. 'What about scary dreams?'

'Those come from our own heads,' says Sister Agnes. 'From our fears, Brian. We can learn a lot from dreams but, unfortunately, the older one gets, the less likely one is to remember them.'

'I always remember mine, Sister,' he says.

'Children are always remembering,' says Sister Mary Clare. 'And it's perfectly normal now, for small children to have nasty old nightmares. You're having a lot of fears when you're little.'

'I'm not little,' he says.

'You'll be a lot bigger yet,' she replies, putting the breakfast cereal and milk back in the chilly bin.

'I remember my dreams,' says Sister Luke. 'Since I've been blind, they've been very vivid, all colours of the rainbow. Compensation, I suppose. God gives and God takes away.'

'I don't get it,' he says. 'Good dreams come from God and bad dreams come out of people's heads. But people come from God. So bad dreams come from God, too, don't they?'

'God is not Father Christmas to fill your stocking with sweets,' says Sister Luke, her hands feeling across the table for dishes to take to the sink.

'That is true,' says Sister Agnes. 'With some questions, Brian, we have to wait for the answers. Bad dreams are like medicine. We don't always understand the benefits until we are older.'

'Benefits?'

'Sure now,' says Sister Mary Clare. 'Everything works for good.'

Sister Luke picks up the toast plate. 'I am the God of good and the God of evil,' she says. 'I create darkness and I make the light. I alone and no other do all these things. That's Holy Scripture from *Isaiah*.' Her other hand closes over the butter container. 'Chapter forty-five, I think.'

Sister Mary Clare waves her hands. 'Sister dear, it's being much too early in the morning for theology. Brian has had the most beautiful dream of his lovely mother and she said his name, and we thank God for that.'

'She said more,' he says. 'She said there's no such thing as dead.'

'Now isn't that the truth!' cried Sister Mary Clare. 'What did I tell you? The very words, Brian. Chickens out of the egg? Himself from the tomb?'

He looks at Sister Agnes, thinking she'll mention something about prisons and windows, but she doesn't say a word. She is putting the cold pads in the chilly bin with the butter and milk.

'Good out of evil,' says Sister Luke, lowering the dishes into the sink. 'Prudence out of virtue. War out of peace and peace out of war.'

'Today, Luke, we'll be seeing Patricia,' says Sister Mary Clare. 'Won't that be grand?'

* * *

Brian is now very confused about the origin of dreams and their meaning but he knows with certainty that his mother was in his dream not as an angel or a candle flame but her real self, leaving his head full of smiles the way aniseed leaves a taste in the mouth. He runs through the motel yard, carrying Sister Luke's pillow and rug, his sandals slapping the concrete and setting up small echoes in the morning. Sister Agnes tells him he is like a dog running twice the distance necessary and he'd better get it out of his system because he's not going to get another chance until they get to Patricia's house in Ashburton, but she says it with a little twitch of her mouth that makes him laugh. Then she tells him it is his turn to sit in the front.

They stop for fuel at a petrol station in the Kaikoura township. Brian knows how to do this. His father showed him. He unscrews the petrol cap and stands on his toes to reach the pump handle.

'Will you look at this boy?' says Sister Mary Clare to the garage man. 'Next thing you know he'll be fixing the motor for us, doing you out of your job, so he will.'

The man smiles, scratches his head and looks over the top of the car to a heap of Christmas trees on a trailer in the next bay. Brian has noticed that some people don't know how to talk to nuns. Sister Agnes passes some money out of the window to Sister Mary Clare, who pays the man and hands back the change while Brian makes sure the petrol cap is fitted tight. It is important to check these things.

'The cost of benzine!' says Sister Mary Clare to Sister Luke. 'When we were young we'd be paying the same for perfume, we would, a little bottle of lily of the valley.'

Perfume, thinks Brian, and his head suddenly floods with the scent from his dreams.

Sister Luke gives one of her barking laughs. 'Oh! Mother Superior sniffing like a bloodhound!' she says. 'Poor Patricia, she was always in Mother's bad books.'

'That wasn't perfume,' says Sister Agnes, moving the station wagon into the street. 'She rubbed geranium on her skin, scented geranium leaves picked from the school grounds. I remember.'

They tell stories about beautiful Sister Patricia until a bus sounds its horn behind them and Sister Agnes has to stop to let it pass. 'Much too fast,' she says, shaking her head. 'I'm not surprised there are so many accidents.' She stirs the gear lever, looking for the right slot. 'Did you see all the people in that bus? St Christopher protect their poor endangered selves.'

Sister Mary Clare says, 'Beauty like that, it was needing marriage to look after it. Or an enclosed order. You wouldn't believe the men now who came back to the faith, lining the pews for the sight of her like a rare rose, and the women liking her because they're after thinking she's out of harm's way.'

'No one was surprised when she left,' Sister Agnes says to Brian.

'Still,' says Sister Luke. 'To wed Davie McCarthy of all people!'

'Oh, but he was a kind man,' says Sister Mary Clare, and they laugh as though kindness is something too funny for words. Brian looks out the window. Sister Patricia might be beautiful but he'll bet anything they like she's not a patch on his mother.

* * *

Nearer Christchurch, Sister Agnes stops in a small town to purchase a newspaper and a bag of peppermints. She passes the peppermints around and gives the newspaper to Brian, telling him to read in a voice loud enough for Sister Luke in the back seat.

'What do you want me to read, Sister?' he asks.

'Anything but the advertising,' says Sister Luke.

'There's something about the Springbok tour.'

'Yes, yes,' says Sister Luke. 'Read that.'

He folds the paper in his lap, picks it up. 'Air Force aircraft and Army trucks will be used to transport police around the country to prevent dis–rup–tion of next year's South African rugby tour.'

'Dear God!' says Sister Agnes.

'The Prime Minister Mr Muldoon said that the Cabinet had proved – no, a–approved additional ex–pend–'

'Cost,' says Sister Agnes.

'Cost–iture for police and defence oper–ations during the tour.'

'We'll be after having a civil war in the country,' cries Sister Mary Clare. 'It'll be a most terrible thing.'

'Go on,' says Sister Luke.

'The Rugby Union's obstin–acy in allowing the Springbok tour to go ahead will cost taxpayers –' He puts his finger on the page. 'What's two with six noughts?'

'Six noughts are a million,' says Sister Agnes. 'You should know that.'

'– taxpayers two million dollars plus a real possibility of strife in New Zealand –'

'What was I telling you?' said Sister Mary Clare.

'– and the loss of our inter–national rep–u–tation for justice and racial equality. That's the view of the Rev. John Murray, spokesman for the joint Metho–dist–Presby–ter–ian public questions comm–it–tee. He said the Churches have worked hard together over the last few – few months –' He looks out the window, sees a tractor in a paddock, cutting hay.

'Don't stop,' says Sister Luke.

'– to persuade both the Rugby Union and the Government in the name of common human–ity to stop the tour.'

'The tour's going to happen,' says Sister Agnes. 'The Rugby Union's holding the country to ransom. There'll be a prayer vigil in every parish.'

Brian looks sideways at her. 'Dad says politics doesn't have anything to do with sport.'

For a second or two no one says anything, then Sister Agnes bunches her hands up on the steering wheel. 'Brian, black children in South Africa are not allowed to play rugby. Only white children can play. Now is that politics or is it sport?'

He looks down at the paper. 'I don't know.'

'Read something else,' says Sister Mary Clare.

He turns the page. 'Crisis deepened by plane-crash deaths. The death of Port–u–gal's Prime Minister Fran–cisco Sa Carn – I can't read this word.'

'Leave that and go on to the next thing,' says Sister Luke.

'Nearly all Oppo-sition parties walked out of the Indian Parl–i–a–ment when Prime Minister Ind–i–ra Gand–hi's Government tabled a Bill which would enable it to arrest people without trial.'

'Enough, enough!' says Sister Agnes. 'What a Job's comforter the newspaper has become! Job was in the Old Testament, Brian. He was a troubled man surrounded by miserable people. But today is a day of celebration and we positively reject it. Do you reject all misery, Brian Collins?'

'Yes, Sister,' he says, wondering what she is talking about.

'Then we shall have nothing but good news,' she says firmly. 'Some jokes or a song, a verse or two of poetry. Do you know Tennyson's "The Brook"? I come from haunts of coot and hern. I make a sudden sally, and sparkle out amongst the fern, to bicker down the valley.'

He looks out the window and sees a line of cars in the wing mirror, and he remembers his parents leading off a dance called the conga which became a long snake of people singing, laughing, weaving from room to room.

'By thirty hills I hurry down and slip between the ridges, by twenty thorps, a little town and half a hundred bridges.'

The noise starts behind them. Honk, honk! Toot! To-o-o-ot!

He remembers that when his mother danced the conga, she was wearing a bright blue dress and red shoes.

'Haste and more haste,' Sister Agnes complains of the drivers who are sounding their horns. 'Where is the pleasure of a beautiful scene if there is no time to enjoy it?'

'Oh Brian,' his mother said in the dream. 'Oh Brian, oh Brian,' and he is sure that if he hadn't woken up when he did, she might have said something about snow on a mountain.

* * *

He didn't know why his father wanted to go to Antarctica in the first place. Dad was not a traveller but a man who took the family to the same holiday bach every January, not thirty kilometres from home. Who told him about the job at Scott Base? What made him leave Mum, four children and a baby and a lump growing that wasn't a baby, to go to a place so cold that your eyebrows turned to ice and broke off against your Polaroids and the wind blew white across white so that you couldn't see where you were going? Was it just the summer job at the Base? Good money, he said. Or was it something inside him like a bird's migratory instinct, the same itch for snow that was in Brian, always quivering like a compass needle? Dad said he would go back tomorrow given half a chance. Would the snow itch get so bad that he'd leave his family with their stepmother, to spend another summer in Antarctica? Brian thinks it could happen and he wonders how old a boy has to be before he can accompany his father to Scott Base.

* * *

He is disappointed that they don't go into Christchurch city. Sister Agnes says that Patricia is expecting them for lunch and they are already late. Perhaps they'll go to Christchurch on the way back, she says. Now they must travel on the bypass road near the airport, pausing occasionally to let a stream of traffic go by. He plays with the seat-belt catch, opens the glove box and looks at the papers inside. Why do they call it a glove box?

'Knock, knock,' says Sister Agnes.

'Who's there?' he says.

'Isobel,' she replies.

He knows it. Every kid has known it for ever. 'Isobel who?' he says.

'Is a bell necessary on a bicycle,' says Sister Agnes, smiling over the steering wheel. 'All right, Brian, what's a theorbo?'

'A what?'

'Theor – bo.'

'I don't know, Sister.'

'It's a seventeenth-century musical instrument like a guitar but much bigger. What's a sackbut?'

'Another musical instrument?' he guesses.

'You're right!' she says. 'It's an early trombone. And a psaltery?'

He looks past her head and sees a range of mountains, green and brown.

'How long before we get there?' he asks.

'When I was young,' says Sister Luke, 'my father had an apothecary shop in Dublin. There were square bottles with glass stoppers, all labelled in black and gold with strange names and even stranger smells. My Da had a white coat with buttons on the shoulder. He made heart pills in a mortar and pestle, dried foxglove leaves, chalk powder. He made tar ointments on a glass slab. Sometimes he let me help him.'

'God be praised!' says Sister Mary Clare. 'In the old days when we be cutting ourselves, it was a cobweb off the side of the house and onto the bleeding, and perchance a spider along with it.'

Sister Agnes turns the car into the side of the road, to let traffic past. 'Does anyone know what a psaltery is?' she asks.

* * *

Sister Mary Clare says that the town of Ashburton is long like a string of pearls. Brian doesn't know the length of a string of pearls but he can see that the town goes on for ages, shops and more shops and, finally, a road of green trees that turns back on itself to reveal wooden houses with fences, lawns, mailboxes. Sister Agnes must stop twice to look at instructions written on the back of last Sunday's Mass newsletter, and then they find it, a pale green house fronted with flowers all the way out to the footpath.

'Oh my,' says Sister Agnes, 'just look at all those dahlias!'

'Dahlias?' says Sister Luke.

'A veritable sea of flowers, Luke,' says Sister Agnes. 'Can this be Patricia's? Yes. Thirty-seven. I didn't know they were gardeners. Stay there, Brian. We'll park in the driveway.' She turns the car and as they drive through the gateway, the front door opens and out comes an old woman with pink fluffy slippers and a purple cardigan. That, thinks Brian, will be Patricia's grandmother. She stands on the porch, laughing and waving her hands as though she's trying to shake something off them.

'We're here!' calls Sister Agnes through her open window.

'God bless us! Patricia!' says Sister Mary Clare.

Brian looks in the garden and towards the garage at the end of the drive. 'Where?'

The grandmother comes down the steps, her arms held wide. 'Agnes! Luke! Mary Clare! It's marvellous to see you.'

Sister Mary Clare is first out of the car, arms ready for the old lady's hug. Sister Agnes turns off the engine and opens her door. Sister Luke fumbles for her seat-belt buckle.

Brian doesn't move. This old woman is Patricia? The famously beautiful Patricia-like-a-film-star? She has thick grey hair, a round face seamed like a pumpkin and folds of skin on her neck that wobble when she kisses Sister Mary Clare, Sister Agnes and then Sister Luke, who is standing at the car door, laughing and saying, 'Make room for Bartimaeus!'

'You've no idea how I've been looking forward to this visit,' says the woman. 'Oh, it's too many years! Agnes, you've lost weight. You look very regal, I must say. Luke! Dearest Luke, has your sight really gone? You were always such a reader. Wasn't she a reader, Agnes? And the embroidery! Mary Clare, you're the one who hasn't changed a scrap. Where's the boy?'

Sister Mary Clare pulls his door open. He is sitting pressed against the back of the seat, his seat-belt still done up. The woman bends over, filling the doorway with her wrinkled smile and purple cardigan.

'This is Brian,' says Sister Mary Clare. 'Brian, meet our dear Patricia.'

Cautiously, he puts his right hand across. 'Hello, Sister Patricia.'

She laughs as she encloses his hand in hers. 'Bless you, Brian, I'm not Sister Patricia. Try calling me Aunty Pat.'

* * *

Her real name, he discovers, is Mrs McCarthy and her husband Mr McCarthy, who used to make kitchen benches and cupboards, is a driver for Meals-on-Wheels and will be back in a couple of hours. They must make themselves at home, she says, and she takes them into a house which is as full of stuff as a souvenir shop, pictures in gold frames, little figures made of china and glass, wooden bowls and cups, crystal dishes, a collection of thimbles, a real hawk stuffed with its wings stretched out, lace covers and cushions, a statue of the Sacred Heart made of white marble. In the corner of the lounge is a Christmas tree with winking lights and behind that, a fat little dog lies asleep on a tartan cover in a basket. Through the double doors and into the dining room, they see a table of food covered with a white net.

First things first, says Sister Agnes, they have the Blessed Sacrament in the car, and Patricia – Mrs McCarthy – says, oh, yes, yes, of course, and she holds Sister Luke's hand as they all go out and bring in Mother Magdala's chest, through the glass front door, right through the lounge and into the back sun room where there are flowers and ferns growing in pots, and Sister Mary Clare says isn't it a lovely place for Himself, and Sister Agnes says yes it is, and Mrs McCarthy cries a bit and tells them it's the first time the Blessed Sacrament has been in her house.

When the cloth comes off the table, it looks like a birthday party with plates of cold beef and chicken, little salads with spoons in them, asparagus from the garden, bread rolls, a chocolate cake, small biscuits iced in pink with half a cherry on top, a jug of lemonade. Brian eats until he is so full that all he can do is pick the cherries off the rest of the biscuits and Mrs McCarthy – Aunty Pat – says that's okay, why doesn't he just go ahead because Mr McCarthy doesn't like cherries, anyway, and after lunch Brian might like to walk around the garden until Mr McCarthy comes home and shows him the workshop. He doesn't go outside. It's more interesting listening, looking at the things in the lounge and patting the dog, who is very old and whose breath smells good and stinky.

The Sisters stay at the table with Aunty Pat, talking about the times gone by and people Brian has never heard of. They laugh so much that sometimes they gasp and wipe their eyes under their glasses and Sister Luke says, oh dear, oh dear, the world is too much with us. Then Aunty Pat wants to know about the sale of the convent, which was, she says, a draughty old barn even in her day, and thanks goodness they've got rid of it.

'Mr Loveridge is such a nice man,' says Sister Agnes. 'He's saving the stained glass window in the chapel. When we buy the house, he'll have one of his men put the window in the prayer room for us.'

'You're buying a house with a prayer room?' says Aunty Pat.

'We'll convert a bedroom,' says Sister Agnes.

'That window was made in France,' says Sister Luke. 'From France to Ireland to New Zealand. The seven pillars of wisdom.'

'Can they get it out without breaking it?' says Aunty Pat.

'Mr Loveridge thinks so,' Sister Agnes replies. 'We're not having a lot of garden, Patricia. My days of gardening are at an end. Who grows those beautiful dahlias?'

'We do. Davie and I. We show them and sell them. It's an interest.'

'Brian is our gardener,' says Sister Mary Clare. 'Sure and he looks young but it's an old head he's having on those shoulders. Back home, we used to say there were folks who never quite came across when they were born. Always one foot in the other world. That's our Brian.'

'He cuts the grass,' says Sister Luke.

'Makes a fine job of the lawns and weeds the vegetables,' says Sister Mary Clare. 'And the flowers. You wouldn't be believing a boy so young with such capable and gifted hands.'

'Indeed,' says Sister Agnes, raising her voice. 'Surpassed only by his capable and gifted ears.'

Brian stops patting the grunting dog. He stands up and goes outside, shutting the door on their laughter.

* * *

137

By the time Mr McCarthy comes home, Brian has worked out what he'll look like, and the small man with the round shoulders and grey moustache does not surprise him as Sister Patricia did. 'So you're the boy who's going to the snow,' he says. 'What's your name?'

'Brian Collins, Mr McCarthy.'

'What are you doing sitting out on the steps?'

'Aunty Pat said to wait for you. She said you'd show me your workshop.'

'She told you that, did she? If you're calling her Aunty Pat, then I'd better be Uncle Dave. What's yours again?'

'Brian.'

'Brian, wait here until I pay my respects. I won't be a jiff.' He goes through the front door, a funny walk as though he's treading water, and is away for ages. When he comes out, he is followed by the fat white dog with the stinky mouth. 'This is Bessie. She's fifteen. That's seventy-five for humans. Have you ever worked a wood lathe?'

'What's that?'

'An idea Aunty Pat has for a boy travelling around the country with three nuns. How are you getting on with them?'

'Good.'

The man pushes his hands deep into his cardigan pockets and scrunches up his mouth. 'Bored out of your tree?'

'No!' He fires the word and then searches for the truth. 'Hardly ever.'

'Hell's teeth, boy, I would be.' The man opens the side door of the garage. 'If I were your age, I'd be running away to sea on the first ship that came along. What'd you say your name was?'

'Brian.'

'Sorry. I forget things, especially the nouns. When you get to my age you'll understand.' The man goes inside the door and puts on some lights.

'I do understand,' says Brian. 'Sister Luke's the same. She forgets. She's got a hole in her brain and the words fall in.'

'A hole? Nobody gets a hole in their brain. Who told you that?'

'Sister Luke did.'

The man grinned. 'Maybe if she said it, it proves it's true. Maybe I've got one and don't know it. You're the kid that's been living at the old convent?'

'Yes.'

'Why?'

Brian looks around at the workroom, long benches, two vices, tools hanging on the walls. The reasons are too complex for a simple answer. He shrugs and then, because the man is still waiting, says, 'I help the Sisters. They think I've got a vocation.'

'A what?'

'A vocation.'

'That's what I thought you said. What kind of vocation?'

Brian looks at the man. 'To be a priest.'

'How old are you?'

'Nearly nine.'

'Son of a gun,' says the man. 'We all go through it, but that's young to be thinking Church.'

Brian doesn't answer. He always has this problem with adults. He thinks it's difficult for anyone to be taken seriously when they look like a little kid.

'Your mother's passed on, hasn't she? Bet you were the apple of her eye. Her favourite, eh?'

He nods, feeling a surprise of tears pricking at his eyes.

'Tough that,' says the man. 'Being the favourite. Tough not being the favourite.' He pulls an oil-stained cover off a machine. 'Boys can never win where mothers are concerned. This contraption is a wood lathe and here's the sort of thing I make on it.' He holds up a bowl of pale wood.

Brian studies the machine bolted to the bench, steel and chipped green paint, bar shining with oil, a silver wheel, an electric cord, a switch. 'How does it work?'

He watches while the man puts on some rough timber the size of a rolling pin with grooves in it, then winds the machine back until the wood is caught, squeezed, skewered. The man puts on goggles, the straps making his big ears stick out further, and switches on the machine, which shudders and hums and spins. 'These are the tools,' he yells. 'The round one is a gouge and the flat one is a chisel. This is the way you hold them, supported like this.' A wisp of wood curls up from the edge of the steel, grows long and falls away. A groove deepens in the timber. 'Do you want to try?'

Now Brian has the goggles and the man's hands are over his, showing him the right way to hold the gouge, how not to hold it, how not to dig it in, lightly, lightly, get the feel of the grain of the wood, that's it, finally the hands falling away from his like learner wheels off a bicycle, and the gouge digging in, bucking, juddering, wood going ragged, no, no, a lighter touch, lightly now, yes, you champion, that's it, a shaving streaming out in a long thin curl, and now he can try a chisel.

Brian's hands are sweating with effort. He wipes them on his shorts, takes the chisel, rests it on the bar, yes, right first time.

'Really easy, isn't it?' says the man. 'Same as any job, you don't force the tools. You let them work for you. Do you want to make a gizmo?'

'What's that?'

He switches off the machine. 'Everyone makes one first time. We'll find a chunk of thick broom handle. Somewhere here. Rimu sapwood, soft, short grain, perfect for a beginner's gizmo.'

He talks to Brian about the grain of wood, how the cells in a tree are long and fibrous to prevent the tree from breaking, and how the wood, growing towards the sun, always reaches back to the earth that feeds it, and if Brian rubs his hand both ways he can feel the difference, the smoothness of wood to earth, the roughness of wood to sky. He cuts the broom handle with a tenon saw. 'I suppose you realise,' he says, 'that there's not much snow around this time of year.'

Brian nods.

'I'd get close to saying there isn't any. Funny time for them to choose. Whose idea was it?'

Brian watches the bit of broom handle going into the lathe. 'I

don't know. They were coming to see Sister Patricia – Aunty Pat –
and they said, they said, I could come too and – and –'

'That a fact? I was under the impression they were bringing you
south to see snow and they were calling here on the way. Bit odd,
we thought. Are you going to the West Coast?'

'Where?'

'Over the other side. Haast – Franz Josef Glacier?'

'No, I don't think so. We've only got four days more.'

'Then you'll be looking for a miracle, boy-oh.'

Brian smiles and nods, pleased that at last the man understands.
'We've been praying about it,' he says.

'Have you now?' the man says.

'Sister Agnes says there will be snow for sure.'

The man tightens the wheel on the lathe. 'That should do it,' he
says. 'Yep. That'll surely do it.'

* * *

The gizmo is about seventeen centimetres long and waisted like a
fancy chair leg, finished with sandpaper, wiped with oil. Brian slaps
it against his left hand and tells Sister Mary Clare he's not sure what
he'll do with it, a candlestick, a handle for something, he'll think
about it, and she, putting down her knitting to look, says it be a
marvellous thing to behold, just lovely, and didn't she always tell
him he could do anything?

Sister Luke is resting and the other three are in the lounge
talking, drinking more tea. The fat hairy dog, which has just
waddled in, collapses with a sigh across Aunty Pat's feet and she
rubs its stomach with her fluffy slippers while she tells them that
she and Dave are going to night classes to learn to make baskets,
and where is Dave now, where is the boy, yoo hoo Brian, how would
you like to go with Uncle Dave to feed the goldfishes in the lily
pond? Brian knows that means she and the Sisters want to talk
about private things like the bishop and the selling of the convent,

which will, according to Aunty Pat, rock the diocesan boat a real treat. So Brian goes back to the workshop, where Uncle Dave is sweeping wood shavings, and he is given a plastic jar of goldfish food and pointed to the back of the garden behind the glasshouse.

The McCarthys have no lawn. Their yard is like their house, stuffed full of interesting things, paths dividing bits of garden, an old wheelbarrow planted with flowers, a fake windmill, a small glasshouse with tomatoes in flower, a tree with fruit like green marbles, a pond with purple blooms around the edge and water lily buds in the middle. The fish come up from the dark water, lots of them, not gold but bright orange and white with working mouths and round eyes that make him laugh because they remind him of Father Friel. When he sprinkles food pellets on the surface they splash and jostle and come right out of the water. He can hear their mouths sucking. This is choice, really cool. Maybe Uncle Dave'll tell him how to make a pond and then he can ask Dad if they can have one in their backyard by the kitchen, as long as Liz's kitten doesn't eat the fish. He throws some more food on the pond to create another frenzy of splashing. Maybe he can get some goldfish for Christmas.

* * *

That night they have sausages because Aunty Pat forgot to take the leg of lamb out of the freezer. At the table, they make jokes about forgetting and Brian is pleased when Sister Luke tells everyone she has a hole in her brain that gobbles up words. That will convince the man – Uncle Dave – that Brian has got it right.

Uncle Dave laughs and says one of the good things about getting old is that you keep meeting new friends, and away they all go again, with Sister Luke holding her serviette up to her lips and Sister Mary Clare's shoulders shaking. Brian looks at them and then at Uncle Dave. Why do they laugh when there's no joke?

'Do you know about the senior citizen who went to memory

school?' says Uncle Dave. 'He was telling his friend what a great school it was, and how it'd helped him, and his pal said, "What's the name of the school?" So the fellow said, "Wait a minute and I'll tell you, there's a flower, it's got a stem about this long, and some thorns and leaves, a very beautiful flower on top, what do you call it?" "You mean a rose?" said his friend. "That's it!" said the man, and he turned and called out, "Rose? Rose? Can you tell me the name of that memory school?"'

They are laughing again.

Brian cuts his sausage in half and pours on a glug of tomato sauce. Mr McCarthy is good at making things but he's totally forgotten what jokes are.

* * *

The Sisters have the extra bedrooms and Brian has an eiderdown on the couch, which is near the Christmas tree and the basket where the fat dog lies grunting and snoring. They put the lights out in the lounge and dining room but if he lifts his head he can see all the way through to the kitchen, where they stand, arms folded, still talking. He can't hear what they're saying. He closes his eyes and next thing, the fat dog is up on the couch, grunting and snorting against the back of his legs. He puts his hand down to pat it and when he sniffs the dog smell on his fingers, he thinks it's exactly like the pong of the goldfish food. There is more laughter from the kitchen. Sister Agnes has her back to the bench beside Sister Mary Clare, who is wearing a blue dressing-gown and a white cap like a baby's bonnet. Aunty Pat, who stands opposite them, has on Sister Mary Clare's veil. She is looking at herself in the darkened window and rocking with laughter.

Brian feels shock. How can that be right? How can it be a joke?

He crawls right down under the eiderdown, feels the dog shift, sigh, settle again, and he shuts his eyes, seeing a blue dressing-gown against his eyelids. Blue dress, he thinks. Blue dress, red shoes, red earrings, oh Brian. He covers his eyes with his hands, surprised at himself. How could it have happened? A whole afternoon and evening have gone by and he hasn't talked to his mother.

* * *

Aunty Pat, who is going to morning prayer with the Sisters in the sun room, tells Brian that if he likes, he can help Uncle Dave set the table for breakfast. Brian says no thanks, he'd rather go to morning prayer, if that's all the same, and she says all right, will he bring in the extra chair from the hall. They have to put on the light in the sun room. There is no sun. The sky is dark grey and rain falls in straight lines against the windows, which Brian takes to be a sure sign from heaven. When they go south the drops of water will turn white and become as light as air, piling up on the windscreen wipers of the car. He knows exactly what it will look like. He has seen it in films. Snow trucks with grader blades will push the whiteness off the road, heaping it up on the sides, and the trees will hold out arms drooping with whiteness like real Christmas trees.

Lord open our lips. And we shall praise your name.

He says sorry to his mother for forgetting and not thanking her for the dream, maybe he's getting a hole too, maybe it's catching, ha ha, only joking, but he knows she won't mind him forgetting because she's happy in heaven, and will she please say thank you to Our Lord and his Mother for sending rain for the beginning of snow and pretty soon, after prayers, after breakfast, they'll be driving south to coldness and mountains and then, and then. Oh yes, and then.

The Saviour of the world will rise like the sun; and he will come into the womb of the Virgin like rain gently falling on the earth.

Oops, he nearly forgot to say that yesterday he made a gizmo and he's going to ask Dad if he can have a goldfish pond when he gets back home.

Who lives and reigns with you and the Holy Spirit, God, for ever and ever, Amen.

CHAPTER ELEVEN

FOR THE FIRST HOUR OF THE JOURNEY THE RAIN IS STRONG, bouncing off the car, the road, the windscreen, and sometimes Sister Agnes has to stop because she can't see clearly. 'It's like being under a waterfall,' she exclaims and then she offers up prayers for the drivers who speed past them. Sister Luke, who is in the front passenger seat, asks Brian if he made a mistake and asked God for rain instead of snow, and although he knows it's a joke, he explains that when they get to Mount Cook, the rain will freeze and make snowflakes, and she laughs saying what a miracle that will be.

As they were backing out of the McCarthy driveway, he thought it strange that Sister Luke, who could see only vague shapes, should sit next to Sister Agnes in the viewing seat, but he soon realises there's not much to see today. It isn't just the rain. The cloud has come right down and is sagging on the trees like an old tent, cutting out so much light that he has difficulty reading the comics Aunty Pat gave him. Sister Mary Clare knits but says she can do this pattern with her eyes closed. For over twenty years, she says, she has made a little jacket for every baby born in the parish. 'Why?' he asks. 'Because every baby is baby Jesus,' she says. He doesn't know how that can be and asks her if it is a parable. She says no it's the truth, and one day she'll be explaining, and he should know that he and his sisters and little Joey all got jackets when they were born, so they did. He gets the heavy feeling of not understanding and goes back to trying to read a comic, leaning against the window and holding the page to his face.

* * *

The rain is lighter at Temuka where they stop for petrol. Sister Agnes takes Brian into a chemist shop to buy him some sunglasses.

'I told you to pack them,' she says. 'I put them on your list.'

'I haven't got any,' he says.

'You could have borrowed some.'

Who from, he thinks. Kathy? Oh yeah, especially after he sat on her last pair at the beach. There were his father's big Polaroid goggles that filled up Brian's face like a swim mask, but no way would Dad lend his Antarctic glasses to anyone.

'I'm sure your father could have bought some for you,' says Sister Agnes. 'He of all people should know the importance of protecting eyes from snow glare.'

'He said there wasn't going to be any snow.'

'Did he indeed?' Sister Agnes is looking at price tags on sunglasses.

'And Mr McCarthy too, Sister. Mr McCarthy said it needed a miracle to get snow this time of year.'

'But we believe in miracles, don't we, Brian?' She pulls out a pair and thrusts them at him, poking the corner of his eye. He takes them from her and fits the arms carefully around his ears. The chemist shop goes dark.

'Yes, Sister.'

'Good. Just keep on praying and leave the rest to God.'

* * *

Dad told him people went blind from snow and it took days for their sight to recover. Brian understood that, the white light getting in behind people's eyeballs and leaking into their heads so it was all they saw, white and more white. When people got caught in a snowstorm, said Dad, they not only lost their sense of direction, they lost a feeling of who they were. They heard voices and music in the snow and it was all so beautiful, they wanted to lie down in it and give themselves up to the whiteness. Brian thinks maybe that's what happened to St Paul. He was Saul then. He was going to Damascus when he was struck by a great white light that made him fall blind off his donkey or horse or whatever it was, and the voice of God came in the whiteness saying Saul, Saul, what the heck do you think you are doing? Maybe it was snowing a great whirling snowstorm on that Damascus Road.

* * *

He doesn't wear his new glasses in the car. They make everything dark the way it is when you run into the house after playing in sunshine and your eyes don't want to change. He folds them carefully and gives them to Sister Agnes to put in the glove box with her driver's licence and the *Holden Station Wagon* manual.

'You did bring a woollen hat and some gloves?' she says.

'Yes, Sister.'

'And thick socks and shoes? You can't go in the snow with sandals.'

'Ah now, Sister dear, don't be bothering the boy.' Sister Mary Clare winks at him. 'I was checking his bag myself before we left and it's all there, the clothes for the snow. If he gets his feet froze, I'll knit him new socks in no time at all.'

He smiles his gratitude towards her and looks out at the rain, which is not changing except to become lighter, more like mist. If anything, he thinks, the air outside is getting warmer and soon he'll have to take off the jersey he put on this morning.

147

We believe in miracles, don't we, Brian? Yes, Sister. Yes, we sure do.

* * *

He closes his eyes and goes to the kitchen at the back of heaven where his mother is showing Mary and Jesus how to dance the conga. Mary's hands are on Mum's waist but Mary is wearing a different kind of blue dress, lighter in colour and going all the way to the floor, and Jesus is holding on to it, Jesus a young boy now, not a man, with a fist full of his mother's blue gown, trying to keep in step and laughing as they go around the table, conga, conga. Brian wants to know about the miracle, snow in summer, is it going to happen, is it? His visit to the snow? The mothers don't hear him. They are singing the conga song, voices floating on laughter like angel feathers, once more around the table, rattling the gold tea cups in their gold saucers. Snow, snow, his heart beats out the prayer to them. Snow, now, no, oh please, oh please, snow. Again around the table they come, so close he can smell the flower scent of his mother, and Mary's perfume like church incense and then the boy Jesus lets one hand go of Our Lady's pale blue gown so he can turn and look at Brian, face to face, eye to eye, jump, step, jump, step, conga, conga, and as he goes past, he winks a huge wink with all the knowing of snow in the universe. Immediately Brian's heart is a rugby ball soaring between the posts. It's a goal! There's going to be snow! And when he opens his eyes there is a small patch of blue sky over the hills, the same colour and size as a fistful of Our Lady's gown.

* * *

They stop for lunch down a side road in a nowhere place, because the ground is covered with flowering lupins. Sister Mary Clare says they are wild flowers but Brian thinks there are too many to have grown by themselves, someone must have planted them. The little folk, says Sister Mary Clare, last night while they were all sleeping in Ashburton, the little folk set the table for their lunch. It's times like this, she says, she wished she owned a camera.

Sister Luke tells Brian she knows what lupins are but will he tell her how many and the colours. He can't count them, he says. He couldn't even run through them. Pink and purple and light purple and cream and white as far as he can see, standing up like a valley full of spears. Then, remembering the beach near Kaikoura, he goes off the road and into the wetness to pick some for her. She holds them in her lap and says thank you.

Sister Agnes gets the chilly bin from the back of the wagon. Aunty Pat has given them sandwiches and chicken pies, the rest of yesterday's chocolate cake, a bottle of lemonade and hot water in a thermos for the Sisters' tea. Sister Mary Clare says the blessing. She takes the flowers from Sister Luke, puts them on the floor, and unfolds a serviette over Sister Luke's lap. 'Chicken pie or tuna sand-wich, Luke dear?'

Sister Agnes bends over the chilly bin, her silver crucifix swinging. 'Who wants tea and who wants lemonade? Brian, slow down! Eat with reverence. Let the bread of thy mouth be as praise to the Lord. Has anyone seen the milk?'

He is now far too hot and must take off his jersey. He pulls it over his head, throws it in the back seat. He picks up his pie, bites again, chews, swallows. 'How far is it now?'

The Sisters always eat slowly, even on a picnic. Sister Agnes smooths creases from her serviette. 'Brian, I am driving as fast as it is humanly safe to go in uncertain weather.'

'I know. I just –' He turns to Sister Mary Clare but she is looking towards Sister Agnes.

'It's the weather, Brian,' continues Sister Agnes. 'But it is clearing. Tomorrow is supposed to be fine. God willing, we'll be in snow tomorrow.'

'I thought –' he scratches his head '– we needed rain. You said, Sister, you said rain turned to snow on the mountain.'

She smiles at him. 'Indeed, yes. There will be fresh snowfalls, Brian, new and sparkling. Old snow is not attractive, believe me. Fresh snow is a beautiful gift from God.'

'Why can't we go today?'

'Clouds, Brian. Too many clouds. We won't even see Mount Cook.'

He finishes the rest of the pie in silence, imagining a steep mountain road with cloud so thick you can't see down the steep drop at the edge. It is true that Sister Agnes is a very careful driver.

'This afternoon,' says Sister Agnes, 'we are going to the Drover Motel on the shores of Lake Tekapo. We have a family unit booked for two nights.'

Sister Luke says, 'When I was a girl there was a heavy snowfall in Dublin. I remember the road was very slippery, and the brewery horse. It was something like a Clydesdale. It had a saddle of white snow on its back. Do you remember that, Mary Clare?'

'Well now, Luke,' says Sister Mary Clare, 'it's not the snow but the frost, I'm thinking, and me milking this warm brown cow on a morning that'd take the fingers right off your hands and then come back for your thumbs. Ah, no bigger than Brian, I was. I put my face right into the warmth of her and my hands, so toasty she was. My breath and hers, making smoke together warm as the milk in the bucket. The name of her escapes me, but when her milk bag was empty we blessed it, Father, Son, Holy Spirit, Amen.' She looks at Brian. 'There were being awful strange creatures with strange curses in those parts. Folks could milk their cows and be getting nothing but milk so sour and bad, not even pigs would drink it.'

'I remember snow when I was a girl in Dublin,' says Sister Luke. 'It was like a saddle on the back of the brewery horse and on the shoulders of my mother's woollen coat. It was very beautiful.'

Brian looks at Sister Agnes, who is cutting the chocolate cake on the lid of the chilly bin. She has never talked to him about her childhood except for that one time in the middle of the night when he dreamed about the lion. There is something he must ask. 'Sister, what if it's cloudy again tomorrow?'

She offers him a slice of cake. 'We'll stay as long as it takes,' she says.

* * *

Although the afternoon remains warm and misty, the scenery changes from flat grassland to stony hills that hint of mountains. There are fewer cars and the human signs that are scattered over the landscape look small and lonely, a wet ribbon of road, a rusty hay shed on a hill, fence posts, telegraph poles. There is hardly any grass, just a few sheep that are the same colour as the earth, and rabbits, so many that as they drive past it seems that the stones are moving. The road is not steep but Brian thinks they must be climbing because the cloud is soon all round them and Sister Agnes has to turn the lights on. Not that car lights make any difference. They have to go even slower. Sometimes it seems that they have stopped and the mist is moving, bringing towards them ghostly shapes that don't form gates or signposts until they are level with the car windows. It's a day, says Sister Mary Clare, made for the trickery of the little folk, and Brian is very glad that he's not out there, walking by himself.

They can't see Lake Tekapo but they have no bother finding the Drover Motel for it comes at them out of nowhere, a big sign above a gate and a gravel turn-off with wet tussock grasses growing each side. They drive so slowly that Brian can hear the turnings of the car's wheels, ticker, ticker, ticker, and eventually, out of the mist, grows a brown wooden building with a glowing orange light that turns out to be the word RECEPTION above a window full of plants in baskets.

* * *

This time there are three bedrooms, one for Sister Agnes, one for

Sisters Mary Clare and Luke and one a prayer room with the tabernacle on a small table by the window. Brian will have the divan in the living room, which suits him because that is where the TV is. He wants to turn it on as soon as they arrive but they tell him he needs exercise, go for a walk, not too far, don't fall into the lake. He doesn't even see the lake. The mist is still thick and he doesn't dare venture beyond the shape of the motel lest the little folk be there with their sly grabbing fingers. He knows that, really and truly, the little folk don't exist in New Zealand but there's no point in taking chances. So he walks on the wet crunchy gravel hitting tall spears of lupins with his gizmo stick until a man's voice yells from the motel, 'Stop that!' then it adds, 'Bloody kids!' He puts the gizmo behind his back and walks on. He wasn't breaking flowers. They were the spears of the little folk. Now there's nothing to do, no lake, no mountain, no snow and he's read all the comics. He goes back to the unit and finds that the Sisters are in the prayer room. Good. He can turn on the TV.

He plans to watch TV again when they go to bed, but before they have finished washing the dishes, his eyes are closing by themselves.

'God bless you, Brian.'

'God bless you, Sister Luke. God bless you, Sister Agnes. God bless you, Sister Mary Clare.'

'God bless you, Brian.'

'Holy angels protect you. Goodnight.'

✳ ✳ ✳

'Brian? Brian?'

It's Sister Mary Clare shaking him and he is warm in the blankets, too hot with sunlight layered over him like extra feather quilts. The room is full of brightness, which is hard on his sleep-soft eyes, and he sits on the edge of the bed, hands over his face, fingers rubbing away the night and its dreaming.

'Brian? There is something most lovely for you to see.'

'Where?'

'Are you awake now? In your pyjamas like you are. I'll show you.' She takes his hand and leads him across the room to the sliding door and out onto the wooden verandah that surrounds the building. He yawns and scratches with his free hand, his eyes slowly taking in the changes. The closeness of the mist has gone and there is a big wet country shining under early sun, stony hills, rocks as big as cars, fan-shaped falls of gravel down to a lake – and then he sees it. In the lake. So big and close that his eyes blink fast at the whiteness of it. A perfect snowy mountain on the water. He looks up. The real thing is further away than its reflection but still closer than any snow he's seen before, a steep white peak that soars up from surrounding hills.

'Mount Cook!' he says.

'The one and the same,' says Sister Mary Clare. 'Now isn't it after being the most lovely and perfect thing you ever set eyes on? The clear sky, now. Would you believe that the angels wore out their brooms sweeping away that mist.'

'Mount Cook!' he says again, his heart beating so fast it might just burst with the brightness.

'I prefer the Maori name,' says Sister Agnes, who is standing in the doorway, holding the little bedside table. 'Aorangi, cloud piercer, chieftain of mountain, companion of God. We thought we'd have morning prayer out here. Take this, will you, Brian?'

He carries the table along the deck and puts it down in front of Sister Luke, who is sitting in one of the wood and canvas chairs.

'Good morning, Brian. Can you see the snow?'

'Good morning, Sister Luke. Yeah, it's cool. It's amazing, Sister. Can you see it?'

'I believe I can but not when I look up.' She points towards the lake. 'Down there, I see something light in the grey. Is that snow?'

'It's water, Sister. The snowy mountain's reflected in it.'

'Is it now? Praise God. Describe it for me, Brian.'

He has found that describing things for Sister Luke is like taking photographs in his memory. The work of labelling each part of a scene leaves it so clearly printed that weeks later he can shut his eyes and see every detail playing in his head like a film.

'The lake is long and kind of narrow. It reaches towards the mountain as though it's trying to grab the reflection. Mostly it's grey. Not one kind of grey, light and dark, and some bits of green and yellow and brown on the hills. No ripples, Sister. The lake's dead calm. It's a funny thing but the mountain is clearer in the lake than it is for real. Just like it's trying to show us a photograph of what it looks like up close.'

Sister Mary Clare comes out carrying the tabernacle. Behind her, Sister Agnes has the Advent candle, the white cloth and the prayer books.

Sister Luke leans forward. 'The sky, Brian. Tell me about the sky.'

'It's kind of light grey but I think it'll go blue.'

'No clouds?'

'No clouds, Sister.'

She smiles and sits back. 'Great is God and greatly to be praised.'

* * *

Brian's father said that people were attracted to snow because it was a metaphor for death, the big white-out. Brian didn't know what metaphor meant, didn't even know if there was a metatwo or a metathree. He told Sister Agnes what Dad had said, and she said that the whiteness of snow reminded people of the white light of God from whom they came and to whom they would return. We are all exiles, she said, waiting our time like the children of Israel in Egypt. He didn't know what an exile was either, but didn't want to ask because Sister Agnes was in one of her schoolteacher moods which could turn awful sharp when someone said the wrong thing. He worked out for himself that snow was probably in the Collins blood going way back, maybe even to the Ice Age which they learned about in school. That would have been in Ireland. He isn't

154

sure that New Zealand ever had an Ice Age. New Zealand and Australia and Antarctica had once been one big continent called Gondwanaland but he doesn't know who called it that since there were no people around when it existed. It kind of broke up and went its separate ways but the boundary lines weren't as clear as cutting paper with scissors. You could tell because there was a bit of Antarctica sitting on the horizon right now, looking at itself in the lake, as white as anything he's ever imagined. There is only one problem. Mount Cook is very steep. Even before the snow starts, the sides go straight up in a series of grey cliffs. Brian doesn't know where the road will be.

* * *

The mountain makes everyone happy. Sister Luke and Sister Mary Clare sing together as they clear the breakfast things from the table. Their old voices are a bit shaky but nice, and the song about an eagle and a rock floats on the sunlight like dust. Sister Agnes comes through, smiling, saying that she is going to the office to see a man about a dog. Brian is puzzled. When his father says that, it means he wants to go to the toilet. Sister Agnes looks at him and explains, 'Phoning to check the weather, Brian.'

He understands. Sister Agnes is a careful driver and although she can see that the mist has gone, she will need to get a weather forecast to make sure.

Sister Mary Clare brings a green plastic sack from the car and tips it up on the verandah. In it are three white plastic parcels tied with string, looking like presents but actually containing the Sisters' old gardening gumboots. It's a wonder to Brian that they are so neat with everything. His own gumboots are stuffed in the end pocket of his bag. Sister Mary Clare tells him he'll need his jersey, his padded jacket, his gloves and hat.

'And don't be forgetting those lovely new sunglasses.'

'They're in the car.'

He dresses quickly, his excitement making him clumsy, and goes out, hot as a biscuit in an oven. Sister Mary Clare laughs, saying praise be, does he want to melt like a little ice-cream, for goodness' sake, why doesn't he just carry his hat and gloves and jacket till they get there?

Sister Agnes comes back from the office. There is laughter everywhere, and haste now, as the Sisters put on their gumboots and carry their grey nylon jackets and gloves to the station wagon.

'We're off to the snow, Brian,' says Sister Agnes, shaking the car key at him.

He is not going to say anything about the steepness of the mountain, or his father's certainty that there are no roads to the snow. But the Sisters are so happy, even Sister Luke, who is often shut off by her blindness, all so excited and sure of snow, that the responsibility of the knowledge becomes a burden to him. As they drive out of the motel and onto the road, the car pointing like an arrow to the mountain, he says to Sister Agnes, in a voice as light as he can manage, 'You know, Mount Cook looks very steep. I don't think the road goes way up there.'

The car fills up with their laughter.

'Bless the boy!' cries Sister Luke.

Sister Agnes says, 'Who was it who said a spiritual journey was like going up a mountain? The further you go the steeper it gets but the wider and better the view. Was that Merton or Teresa of Avila?'

'I think it could have been the Dalai Lama,' says Sister Luke, and again they go into laughter.

Brian is sure they have misunderstood. 'Do you really think the road goes as far as the snow?'

Sister Agnes has a tear running into the creases below the hinge of her glasses. She breathes deeply and places her hands more firmly on the top of the steering wheel. 'We believe in miracles, Brian,' she says. 'God willing, we'll go to the snow.'

Yes, of course, miracles. But he knows now that prayers get muddled and miracles have a habit of shifting sideways into something different. The mountain, sitting in the middle of the windscreen, seems to be taunting him, here's my snow, Brian Collins, dare you come and get it, and when he closes his eyes, his mother in heaven is so far away that he can't see the blue of her dress or the red of her shoes, or Our Lady and her Son. The only thing is the mountain, as steep as the wall of a building.

* * *

They don't drive to the mountain. Sister Agnes puts on the indicator, flick, flick, flicking the meaning of the miracle long before she makes the turn into the airport. Brian sits forward in the seat-belt, like a dog straining against its leash. Between some sheds and the hills is a long grey runway with a little plane sitting to the side of it. He has never been in a plane that small. It will take them directly to the snow. The wave of excitement rises up and then falls back without breaking. It's not a ski plane. It has ordinary wheels which means that they won't be able to land. They'll just fly over it. As he suspected, the miracle has shifted sideways, giving a little, taking back some. He is disappointed but knows he mustn't let it show.

* * *

They park by the airport terminal and go in, carrying their winter clothing. Brian has on his new sunglasses. Sisters Agnes and Mary Clare have clip-ons over their ordinary spectacles. They walk over carpet in their gumboots to the counter, where Sister Agnes asks to see Mr Clement Abernathy.

'Sure,' says the woman. 'You are?'

'The Brian Collins group,' says Sister Agnes, opening her handbag on the counter. 'The nine-thirty flight.'

'Right you are,' says the woman, marking their names in a book. 'Clem? You there, Clem? They're here.'

A tall man appears from the office at the back, about as old as

Brian's father but almost bald, round cheeks dark with beard shadow, a lower lip that sticks out. He wears an orange flying suit. 'Sister Agnes!' He goes straight to her and shakes her hand.

She laughs. 'Little Clement! Look what the years have done to you.'

'You haven't changed,' he says. 'Still handing out detentions like there's no tomorrow?' He writes in the air. 'I must not talk in class. I must not talk in class.'

She takes a step forward and pinches his cheek as though he is just a little kid. 'Clement Abernathy, you were such a scamp. I despaired of teaching you anything, and here you are!'

'Ready to put your life in my hands,' he says, holding his big hands out to her.

'Your brother Leo was the scholar. You were greatly interested in sport, I remember.'

'And girls, Sister.'

'And girls,' she says. 'Always something of a Don Juan, although Leo tells me you've finally been caught. An Oamaru girl, Leo says.'

The man's face folds up into creases. 'There wasn't much point in waiting for you, Sister, was there? Yep, I married Sharon Connor from over that way. We've got a six-week-old boy, Timothy. How's Leo?'

'Haven't seen him since I phoned you. They're busy. Three children and they're having alterations done to the shop to include a café – but I told you that.' Sister Agnes turns. 'Do you remember Sister Luke? Sister Mary Clare?'

He comes out from behind the counter to shake their hands.

'This,' says Sister Agnes, 'this is Brian Collins. Brian, meet Clement Abernathy, ex-pupil and pilot.'

'Ah! So you're the one,' says the man, bending to look at Brian, eye to eye. 'Does she teach you, too?'

Brian shakes his head.

'That's something to be thankful for,' the man says.

'Clement, I've been away from school for eighteen years,' says Sister Agnes. 'You can save your blarney. I told you about Brian.

He's my nephew's boy. He's been gardener, mower of lawns and general handyman at the convent without receiving a penny in wages. Nor does he expect any. His reward will be in heaven. But we thought, we might give him a little down payment.'

The man lifts his arms in a helpless gesture. 'I'm sorry I can't do it for nothing,' he says. 'It's a company machine.'

'I wasn't implying you should, Clement,' says Sister Agnes. 'Of course we'll pay our way.' She opens her handbag wider and reaches inside it. 'But I must say we do appreciate the offer of a discount.'

There is money to be counted and papers to be filled in. Sister Mary Clare helps Brian back into his jacket. He does up the zipper, puts on his hat and gloves, feels his body temperature rise. He wonders how people get on in space suits on the moon. What happens if they itch and have to scratch?

'This way,' says Clem, taking them behind the counter and through the office. He opens the outside door. 'There she is,' he says.

It's not the plane he's pointing at. It's a helicopter sitting on the concrete pad like a big red dragonfly. Brian sucks in his breath, eyes widening to take in every part of it. They're going in a helicopter, a real chopper which can, which can, can't it?

'Move, Brian,' says Sister Agnes.

'Can it land on snow?' he asks.

'You betcha,' says Clem. 'It's a great day for the mountain. We'll go up to the head of the Tasman Glacier and I'll let you out.'

'Brian is sitting in the front,' says Sister Mary Clare.

Clem looks at Sister Mary Clare. 'Sorry, Sister. You'll be in front. The three smaller bods have to go in the back.'

Sister Mary Clare looks disappointed for Brian but he grabs her hand. 'It doesn't matter, Sister. I don't mind.' Which is true. Nothing in the entire world matters except this moment and the way it is leaning towards the mountain. 'I'll be able to see. There are windows in the back.'

The front seat is folded down and Brian is lifted in first so that he can help Sister Luke, who is guided from hand to hand until she is in the back seat beside him, laughing and straightening her veil.

After her comes Sister Agnes and the three are squashed in a tight row, with Clem showing them how to fasten their seat-belts. Then he puts the front seat back in place and helps Sister Mary Clare into it. He gets in the pilot's side. The doors are shut. There is more fastening of safety belts.

Clem says, 'It'll take a few minutes to warm up. Once the engines start, we won't be able to talk. Keep your harness done up until we get there and when you get out, don't go near the back of the chopper. Got that? Stay away from the back. There's a little rotor that'll take your head off in a blink. Okay? All happy? Snow, snow, here we go.' He puts on headphones, turns switches, taps a dial. There is a whining noise that coughs, breaks, coughs again, gets higher in pitch, becomes a roar. Chuffa, chuffa, chuffa, chuffa. The blades are turning and picking up speed and the machine shakes all over as though it is impatient to be going. But they must wait and wait. Sister Luke reaches for Brian's hand. Even through two thicknesses of gloves, he feels bones and a soft trembling that isn't the machine.

* * *

He imagines that they are all climbing the mountain, not in a helicopter but real like in the movies, and he is holding Sister Luke's hand, helping her up the rocks to the snow, telling her where to put her feet and describing what the ground looks like far below, the road and river like two little threads, the car like an ant, the airport a button, and in front of them, snowflakes as big as Christmas tree decorations. Don't be afraid, he is telling Sister Luke as they climb from ledge to ledge, this is the miracle mountain, the cloud piercer, the companion of God, we don't need a road because we have the snow to tell us how far we've come, just hold my hand.

* * *

The helicopter shudders, moves sideways like a crab, then forward. They have lifted off and are climbing over the airfield, moving above the river that is strung in curves and loops across grey stones. There is flat land to the left, steep cliffs to the right. They are moving faster. Brian leans forward to see between Clem and Sister Mary Clare and discovers they are not going directly up the mountain but to the side, following the river, which is now a mere crack in a wasteland of grey, stones, rocks, nothing growing. The machine keeps climbing and then, in a shadow, he sees a patch of white. They are over it before he can identify it. White and dirty around the edges. Was it snow? Ice? He sees another patch almost as dark as the rocks that surround it, but with a white glimmer at its heart. He leans further forward.

Sister Luke's grip on his hand tightens. He looks at her and sees that her lips are moving but he doesn't know if she is praying or talking to him. He tries to shout something about the grey stones and patches of white but the engine noise gobbles up the words as they leave his mouth. He smiles widely at her, knowing she can't see, but there is nothing else he can do, and she is now shaking all over as though she is cold. Sister Agnes knows it. She takes Sister Luke's other hand, at the same time giving Brian a look that tells him not to worry. In another second the light in the helicopter changes. Everything outside has turned to a whiteness that is pouring itself in on them. He gasps at the size of it. It's everywhere! Snow! Real snow! He wants to put a size on it but doesn't know how snow is measured. Hectares? Tonnes? Millions of litres? The number of snowflakes falling over hundreds of thousands of years? He knows his mind won't stretch to any figure needed. The snow outside is measureless.

The helicopter goes straight up a sheer snow cliff which rises only metres from the front window, and then they are at the top and sweeping over a valley whiter than a bowl of meringue. They go lower, hover, and he sees small white flurries set up by the wind from the blades. Slowly, the machine settles and its voice drops from a roaring to a rumble.

Clem puts his seat forward and lifts Brian out first. He carries him beyond the helicopter and puts him down in the snow. Brian sinks to his ankles and for a moment stands where Clem has placed him, his arms spread out, his mouth open. He turns his head, following the curved line where blue meets white, all the way around and then down to his shoes, which are almost buried. He lifts a foot, puts it down. The snow is soft. It's like powder, like sand, like sugar, like, like – he doesn't know. All the snow words he has collected from his father's photos are useless, melted to nothing against the real stuff. He takes another step, leans forward, goes down on hands and knees. Snow has a voice. Not a squeak, not a crunch but something like it, a small bird perhaps. There are crystals on his woollen gloves as fine as tiny feathers. He pulls the gloves off and plunges his hands into the white powder, comes up with a mushy heap which he tosses into the air. It falls in his face and he laughs. He takes off his sunglasses. At once the white becomes diamond fire that makes him blink and screw up his eyes. Ha ha, says the snow. You want to see what I really look like, do you? He rubs the glasses on his jacket, puts them back on, puts on his gloves. Then he gets up, runs, staggering, breathless, every footfall a small dark cave. 'Yaa-aa-aa!' he yells at the skyline. 'Yah-yah-yah!' at the Sisters getting out of the little red helicopter. 'Yo! Yah! Yee-ee-ee!'

His voice goes all the way around the valley and comes back as a little white ghost. Yo! Yah! Yee-ee-ee!

* * *

Sister Mary Clare says everyone in snow for the first time must be building a snowman and they should start it right here and now, and Brian discovers that when you get a ball of snow and squeeze it really hard it becomes an iceball. When you squeeze it half hard, you get it about right for making a body with arms at the sides and a head with a knobbly nose. When you hardly squeeze it at all and it's smooth on the outside and soft in the centre, and then you throw it, it explodes and spatters white all over grey cloth.

'Ooh!' shrieks Sister Mary Clare. 'You little spalpeen, Brian Collins, frightening the living daylights out of me! I'll get you!'

Then it's a big snowfight with Sister Mary Clare and Sister Agnes throwing snowballs at him and each other, and he is pelting them and just about falling over with laughter when he gets them or when snow breaks over him like a wave. Clem the pilot stands by the helicopter watching and smoking a cigarette. Sister Luke is still patting snow on the snowman.

'Sister Luke!' calls Brian.

She raises her head.

'See if you can throw a snowball at me. I'll talk. You aim at my voice.'

She smiles, shaking her head.

'Go on. See if you can get me. Just get some snow and squish it in your hands. Bet you know how to do it, Sister. When you were a little girl in Dublin. Bet you made snowballs?'

She bends over and scoops up a handful, moulds it.

'Can you see the snow, Sister? Can you see the light of it? I can't look at it without dark glasses. I'm in front of you – about eight metres.'

She throws.

'That went over my shoulder, my right shoulder. Try another one. Just aim straight at my voice. I'll talk about it. I'll describe it. We're in a kind of valley. The sky is blue, Sister. The snow is around us in wavy white hills and the helicopter is bright red. What else is there?'

She raises her hand over her shoulder and launches another snowball, which falls short. He takes two steps forward.

'Missed. Try again and I'll keep talking, but I don't know what to say. Tell you what, Sister, I'll sing. This is a song from the school concert. O come all ye faithful, joyful and triumphant, o come ye, o come ye to Bethlehem. Come and adore him, born the king of angels. O come let us adore him. O come let us –'

Splat!

'You got me! You got me right in the face!' He runs to her, kicking up snow and laughing. He reaches out, hugs her. Her jacket is open and he feels the cold burn of her crucifix against his face. 'A bull's-eye, Sister! You got me a real bull's-eye.'

She puts her hands on his shoulders, smiling. 'Great is God and greatly to be praised,' she says.

* * *

Clem tells Sister Agnes that they have all behaved like unruly kids and he should give them detentions for getting the inside of his helicopter wet but seeing she was his favourite teacher, he'll let her off this one time, and they'd better come into the office because there'll be mugs of hot chocolate waiting and they can dry off by the heater.

They are still laughing and trembling with the wonder of snow as they walk towards the building. Brian has taken off his gloves and stuffed them in his jacket pocket. His jacket doesn't feel all that damp but his jeans are soaked and clammy against his legs. The hems of the Sisters' habits are as wet as if they have waded across a creek.

Sister Luke pauses by the office door, her hand over her crucifix. She is tired, she tells them, all this excitement, and if they don't mind, she'll go back to the car and rest. 'The brewery horse,' she says, smiling.

Sister Mary Clare wants to go to the car with Sister Luke.

'No, no, the boy.' Sister Luke waves her hand. 'No snowballs, this time, I promise, just my afternoon nap.'

Sister Agnes gives Brian the car keys. He puts his other hand on Sister Luke's arm and guides her carefully around the side of the airport building and across the car park. He holds open the station wagon door while she slides in, feeling the seats with her hands. Her pillow and rug are behind the seat. She shrugs her arms out of her nylon jacket while he fetches them, and gives him the damp jacket

164

which he folds over the back of the seat. He puts the pillow under her head and the rug over her knees. Then he closes her door, goes around the other side, and sits next to her.

'Off you go,' she says. 'It's chocolate.'

'I don't want any.' He drops his own jacket on the floor.

'I'm going to have a nap. You'll be fidgeting like a flea in a fit.'

'No, I won't.' He sits back and folds his arms.

She sighs, closes her eyes, then in a little while opens them and frowns at him. 'Use a fork to make an omelette,' she says, 'not an egg-beater. Remember that.'

'Yes, Sister,' he says.

* * *

It's not difficult to sit still. He is hushed by snow, filled with it as with a three-course Christmas dinner and barely able to move. In the windscreen sits Mount Cook, grey and white, sharp against the sky and distant. They were up there. Yes, they were! For a little while, he doesn't know exactly how long, the mountain opened up all its secrets of snow and now it is closed again, as tight as a lily bud in the McCarthy's pond. We went to the snow, he will tell his father, and it wasn't terrible. It chirped and shook its feathers over us and when we threw snowballs, it sang joyful and triumphant, and although it was big, bigger than anything, and very cold, there was nothing to be afraid of because it was glad. Yes, that's it. It was glad to see us.

* * *

Sister Luke is asleep when the others come back, nested in her pillow and snoring lightly through her thin nose. Sister Mary Clare and Sister Agnes are carrying their jackets and have taken off their sunglasses. They are talking, their heads leaning together. As they get in the car, they look at Sister Luke and lower their voices. Sister Agnes says to Brian, 'Well? Was it the miracle you expected?'

'Better, Sister!' He leans forward. 'Much, much better. It wasn't a miracle though, was it? You got it all planned.'

'Ah, sure now,' says Sister Mary Clare. 'Everything is a miracle.'

Sister Agnes turns around in the driver's seat. 'What do you mean, it was all planned?'

'The pilot. The helicopter. You know.'

She taps with one finger on the back of the seat. 'Brian, miracles are just little doors opened by God. If we don't go through them, nothing happens. I might add that the prompting to go through them is in itself a miracle. Do you understand me?'

He shakes his head.

'It was a miracle that Mr Loveridge's office should be next door to Leo Abernathy's book shop and another miracle that Leo should mention his brother Clement with a helicopter business at Mount Cook. It was yet another miracle that sent us to Mr Loveridge in the first place, a small boy praying that our convent would be made new. Why not, we thought. Why indeed not?'

'It all came together most beautifully in the one day,' says Sister Mary Clare. 'That's why we asked you to choose the car for us.'

'The car?'

'Indeed,' says Sister Agnes. 'The trains don't come here and it's too far to walk. Besides, we wanted to see Patricia.'

'But it might have been an awful car,' he says. 'It might have been a real old bomb that broke down.'

They smile, and Sister Mary Clare waves her hand. 'Ah, we prayed about it,' she says.

* * *

Sister Luke is still fast asleep when they reach the Drover Motel. Sister Agnes says they should not disturb her. They will park the car in the shade and go inside to get the lunch ready and Brian will change out of his wet shoes and jeans and then set the table. It'll be Patricia's egg and asparagus tart.

He puts on his shorts and sandals and hangs his jeans over the railing on the deck. The mountain is reflected in the lake but slightly blurred now with wind ruffle, and nearer the shelter of the motel some water birds are swimming, leaving long ripples behind them.

The table is set and he is sent out by Sister Mary Clare to see if Sister Luke is awake. She isn't. He goes back in, they sit down, and Sister Agnes blesses the meal, a long grace that says thank you for the snow and the helicopter ride and Clement Abernathy and Clement's wife Sharon and their baby and the delicious food provided for them by Patricia. Brian is given the last of the lemonade. Tea is made. Bread is buttered. Sister Luke's portion of the asparagus tart is put on a plate in the warming oven.

Afterwards, he asks if he can watch TV. Sister Agnes says, yes but only for a little while. When Sister Luke wakes up, she'll have her lunch and then they'll all go for a walk by the lake. There are ducks down there. Brian might like to feed them the stale bread.

He turns on the TV and sits on the divan, a cushion on his lap. There are only two channels, a boring film with people talking and kissing, and a soccer match from another country with teams he doesn't know. But he watches the match anyway, his vision drifting off every now and then, to snow. The Sisters wash dishes and go out. He thinks they may have gone to the lake without him, for they're away a long time. It's only minutes to the end of the game and he's about to go out to look for them, when Sister Mary Clare comes in, her face bright red from the sun. She sits on the divan beside him and looks at the TV, then she pulls a handkerchief out of her pocket and blows her nose. He glances at her and is surprised to see that she is crying.

'Brian, there is something to be telling you.' She takes off her glasses and wipes her eyes. 'Something very beautiful and very sad. Praise be to Himself, our dear Sister Luke has gone to God.'

CHAPTER TWELVE

AS THEY CARRY HER TO THE UNIT IN A CANVAS DECK-CHAIR, HE remembers that people said the same thing about his mother, gone to God, gone to Heaven. That knowledge occupies a small part of his thinking, while the rest of him knows that Sister Luke is simply having her afternoon rest. She doesn't look any different. As they walk one on either side of the chair, her head nods slightly and her legs wobble. First one gumboot falls off, then the other, and although Sister Agnes and Sister Mary Clare put the chair down several times, to rest, they don't pick up the boots. Brian wonders if he should try to help but senses there is no room in this for him. The chair is set on the verandah while Sister Agnes straightens, stretches, rubs her back. Sister Luke's head moves further towards Sister Mary Clare and her veil goes slightly askew. Her eyes are shut, her mouth open, her face relaxed in sleep as simple as buttered toast. Behind them, the mountain stands clear and sharp with sunlight, combings of cloud above it. The ordinary quacking of ducks comes up from the lake. They lift the chair and Sister Luke's hands fall out of her lap, and hang down, pale fingers at the edge of her sleeves. It is nothing, thinks Brian. This morning everything happened. They were on the mountain, halfway to heaven. Now they are back and resting and Sister Luke's lunch is in the oven.

Through the door, they lift again, holding the wooden arms of the chair and walking sideways. Brian thinks they will take her to the bedroom and lay her on the bed, but no, it's the prayer room. They set the chair in front of the tabernacle and straighten her in it, feet, hands, head.

'Do you want me to get her rug?' Brian offers from the doorway.

Sister Agnes gives him an odd look, almost as though she hasn't seen him before. 'Will you leave us, please?'

Sister Mary Clare comes to him and stands with one hand on the door so that he can no longer see into the room. 'It be a special time of prayer, Brian. Why don't you go down to the lake and feed bread to the ducks.'

'Which bread, Sister?'

'Any. It doesn't matter. Ah, and Brian?'

'Yes, Sister?'

Her pink eyes swell with tears. 'While you're there, be saying a thank you to God for dear Sister Luke.'

* * *

He takes one slice of bread from the loaf in the chilly bin but it isn't enough. The ducks shovel up the crumbs and surround him, shaking their tails and demanding more. When they see that he has none, they waddle to the water, muttering. He doesn't want to go back to the unit yet. He sits on the stones, thinking about the morning in sequence so that he won't forget any detail when he's telling his Dad. The trouble is, he can't find words to match the experience. Anything he can say about the mountain and the snow doesn't get anywhere near it. There should be new words, ones so special that people could use them only once or twice in their lives.

A warm breeze touches his arms and legs on its way to the lake.

There are no reflections now, just smudges of colour in the ripples, and the mountain at the head of the valley is wearing some cloud around its shoulders. He remembers that he promised to say a prayer of thanks for Sister Luke but when he starts the morning comes back, the snowball exploding in his face and he running to her, using the hug to wipe the snow off his sunglasses.

* * *

Sister Mary Clare comes down to the lake, red-eyed and smiling, and holds out her hand to pull him to his feet. 'Don't be sad, Brian. It was a lovely passing.'

He is not sad. He walks with her towards the motel and as they pass the garden, he sees lupin flowers bent over and broken and he tries to remember who told him lupins were wild things, not planted by anybody. It was misty. He couldn't see. Anyway, he's already decided to give the gizmo stick to his father for Christmas.

'Sure now,' says Sister Mary Clare, 'there be something we always do. Always the vigil of rejoicing when one of our Sisters goes home. At least one of us beside her day and night. Is there any television now you'd want to be seeing?'

He shrugs, not knowing what to say.

She puts her arm across his shoulders. 'Ah, it couldn't have been lovelier. Dear Sister Luke, the heart in her so belonging to God, it's been trying to get there for years. No more pain and pills.' She squeezes his arm. 'Would you believe she's telling your lovely mother about the snow fight this morning and your mother, there, is asking all about you.'

He asks, 'Sister Luke's eyes, are they all right now? Can she see?'

'Sure, and better than any of us. There'll be nothing at all now she can't see and understand.'

So that was it, he thought, another sideways miracle. 'When are we leaving?'

'This very night, Brian. We're needing to get our dear Sister back to the parish and it's a long road to the ferry.'

He thinks of the boat and Sister Luke's face turned to the cries of the gulls and the dolphins leaping from the water. 'That's not for three days.'

'It was, it was, but Sister Agnes phoned and changed the reservation to tomorrow evening's sailing. We'll be sleeping a little and then on our way. Say a prayer, Brian, for strength in Sister Agnes, for I'm after being as useless in the driving a car as a cow is in the flying.'

* * *

Sister Agnes comes out of the room and asks him if he would like to join them for evening prayer. He nods, tired of the company of television and glad that he is not being completely shut out of the prayer room. It is still light outside but his candle is burning beside the tabernacle on the small table covered with the white cloth and in front of it sits Sister Luke, her chin resting on her collar. Her mouth is now closed. There is some kind of bandage under her jaw. She is wearing her gold-rimmed glasses and her black-laced shoes. Her hands are in her lap, one placed over the other, her beads wound around them.

Three more deck-chairs have been brought in from the verandah. His is next to Sister Agnes. Sister Mary Clare sits on the other side of Sister Luke.

In the name of the Father, the Son and the Holy Spirit, Amen.

Moving his eyes under their half-shut lids, he can see Sister Luke clearly, the light of the candle making a shine on her face. It's that and the stillness he notices, no moving lips, no click click of beads.

But she could be praying. She could be asleep. She doesn't look – dead.

My soul glorifies the Lord, my spirit rejoices in God, my Saviour. He looks on his servant in her lowliness; henceforth all ages will call me blessed.

171

He closes his eyes tight, trying to see snowballs and Sister Luke laughing with her face up and her arm over her head, ready to throw. But the laughing face that comes to him is his mother, swirling blue and red and saying oh Brian, there is no such thing as dead, and before he can stop himself, he is crying in the middle of evening prayer, although he feels no sadness, none at all.

On this mountain, the Lord of hosts will prepare for all peoples a banquet of rich food. On this mountain he will remove the mourning veil covering all peoples, and the shroud enwrapping all nations, he will destroy Death for ever. The Lord will wipe away the tears from every cheek; he will take away his people's shame everywhere on earth, for the Lord has said so.

CHAPTER THIRTEEN

HE THINKS HE HASN'T BEEN ASLEEP BUT WHEN HE OPENS HIS eyes, he realises he's been dreaming. Sister Agnes is bending over him, the kitchen light bright behind her, and Sister Mary Clare is filling a water bottle at the sink.

'Brian, it's time to go.'

His eyes are heavy. He can barely move.

'Poor boy,' says Sister Mary Clare. 'Two o'clock in the morning is no decent time to be waking a child.'

'Get dressed,' says Sister Agnes. 'You can go back to sleep in the car.'

He puts his feet over the side of the divan and scratches his arms, his mind vacant. Then it comes back to him, a red helicopter, snow, and he smiles.

He thinks he might see the mountain but there is nothing out there, just a few stars like bits of broken glass in the blackness. The station wagon is alongside the verandah and Sister Luke is in the front passenger seat, her head on her pillow, which is up against the door. Sister Agnes turns off the motel lights and there is only the pale moon wash of the Holden's headlights to guide them down the steps. Brian stumbles against Sister Mary Clare, who takes him by both arms and steers him into the back seat. Then she gets in herself and tucks a rug around him. He suspects it's Sister Luke's rug but is too tired to think about it. He closes his eyes as his head slides against Sister Mary Clare. She is saying to Sister Agnes, 'I praise God for the gift of her hands, the most beautiful fancywork to behold. Do you remember, Agnes, the alb for Father Perry's ordination? Stitches so fine you'd be needing a magnifying glass to see them. Remember the way she used to read to us at mealtimes?'

'They say,' replies Sister Agnes, 'that the last gifts God gives us are patience and forbearance. Dear Luke, she had those in abundance.'

Their voices, and the sound of traffic rushing past, get mixed up with his dreams. He thinks that he's in bed but realises that he's uncomfortable and can't sraighten his legs. He kicks, wriggles, wakes up with his face pressed against the back of the seat and his mouth dry. They are still talking about Sister Luke but now the car is bright with sunlight. In front of him is the edge of Sister Luke's veil folded in a crease on her pillow. Next to her, Sister Agnes drives with hands on the top of the wheel. Sister Mary Clare is nodding over the knitting in her lap. When he sits up, she turns her head and smiles a good morning.

'What's the time?' he asks.

Sister Agnes answers. 'It's a little after half-past nine. Do you want a rest room?'

He feels the inside of his mouth with his tongue. 'I'm thirsty.'

'We'll stop soon,' says Sister Agnes. 'We need petrol for the car and some breakfast.'

Sister Mary Clare has in her knitting bag the lemonade bottle filled with water. She passes it to him and he drinks, looking at houses with trees and gardens and some kids jumping skateboards on the pavement. This time yesterday they were getting into the red helicopter.

'Where are we?'

'The little road behind Christchurch city,' says Sister Mary Clare, taking back the water bottle. 'We're after making good time, praise God, with our Sister Agnes driving so beautifully all through the night.'

Sister Agnes lifts a hand from the wheel and drops it again. 'I would be able to praise God more eloquently if we had another driver,' she says.

Sister Mary Clare puts the cap back on the water bottle. 'Sure now, we're all looking forward to a little stop.'

Soon after, they come to a petrol station and Sister Agnes stops at the edge of the courtyard while they take it in turns to use the rest rooms. Brian glances at Sister Luke and thinks she is looking a bit different now. Her skin is a grey colour and there are tiny black lines on her cheeks and nose.

Sister Agnes drives to the pumps. She says she will stay in the car while Brian and Sister Mary Clare go into the shop to see what can be bought for breakfast.

Brian chooses a can of orange soda from the drinks fridge and Sister Mary Clare groans, 'My tongue is fair hanging out for a cup of tea and a decent sandwich.' But there is no tea in the place, nor coffee either, and they must settle for cans of drinks and three hot meat pies.

A man with khaki shorts and grey hair is filling the car with petrol while Sister Agnes sits sideways, her door open, her handbag on her lap. The man puts the pump nozzle back and closes the petrol flap on the car. Brian sees the way he looks down into Sister Agnes's open bag.

'We got pies, Sister,' says Brian.

'Oh. Well, that'll have to do,' says Sister Agnes, counting money into the man's hand.

He can't take his eyes away from her handbag. 'Going far?'

'To the Picton ferry,' she replies.

'Your friend's having a good sleep,' he says.

Sister Agnes nods as she closes her bag. 'The sleep of heaven,' she says.

'Wake her up when you get to Amberley,' says the man. 'They're having a Christmas festival. Decorated floats and vintage cars. You interested in vintage cars? Father Christmas for the kid? Can't sleep through that. Plenty of parking down the back streets.'

Sister Agnes puts her handbag down by her seat. 'Our Sister has gone to God,' she says in her schoolteacher voice.

The man smiles for a moment, nods and then he has another look at Sister Luke. His eyes get wider, his smile disappears. 'Jesus Christ!'

Oh, thinks Brian. Blasphemery, blasphemery!

But Sister Agnes simply pulls her skirts around her. 'Mind how you use the Holy Name,' she says and closes the door.

* * *

They come to Amberley with its main street full of people, some in fancy dress, a huge Christmas tree covered with decorations, a brass band, lots of old cars. Brian wishes they could stop, maybe just for five minutes, but Sister Agnes drives on and he has to be content with kneeling on the seat and looking out the back window. He stays kneeling because he can see everything, the back of the wagon with the bags and Mother Magdala's chest, the traffic that follows them, a red Rover, a Honda Civic, a small Nissan truck, a tanker behind that, and the road that flows away into the distance. If he looks down, there is a place behind their wagon where the road melts and becomes a river. He imagines that theirs is the last car left on solid land and that the cars following have outboard motors driving them through the grey current. He wonders if anyone has invented a car that can go into the water and be a boat and then take off like a helicopter, and thinks how neat it would be to go from road to sea to mountain all in the one vehicle. Then he realises that there is a blue car with flashing lights coming up fast on the wrong side of the road. He drops back into his seat to do up his seat-belt.

The car draws up alongside them, but doesn't pass.

'Blessed Saints, what does he think he is doing?' says Sister Agnes.

Brian looks at the man in the blue shirt. 'It's a cop, Sister,' he says.

A siren goes on, so sudden and loud that the station wagon lurches. Sister Agnes moves her hands on the wheel. 'I think he's wanting us to stop,' she says.

CHAPTER FOURTEEN

THERE WAS NOTHING URGENT TO KEEP HIM AFTER SCHOOL. He left soon after the students, the manuscript in his backpack with a clutch of assignments on social order in the late twentieth century as interpreted by the New Zealand novel. He doubted that he'd be marking papers that evening.

His mountain bike consumed the distance between school and home in less time than the car, mainly because of the short cut through the park, giving him the added pleasures of sounds and smells which a vehicle denied. It was when he rode his bike that his mind was most productive, responding to external stimuli with involuntary word bursts that seemed to shape themselves. He almost never created poems in the car. That his creative energy was low today was largely due to his irrational disappointment at the rejection of his story script. His over-reaction had become a burden of cringe, now anthropomorphised to a miserable imp that sat in his backpack moaning and wringing his hands. One of Sister Mary Clare's little folk. He grinned at the image and then stood on the pedals to expunge it.

The problem with non-fiction was that it never had an ending.

A poem had its completion at birth. With a true story it was a matter of arbitrary severance as easy or as difficult as taking scissors to a page. He could have gone on with episodes largely filled by his father and Liz, how Sister Agnes and Sister Mary Clare had refused to leave the departed Sister Luke, and how the need to be with their Sister until her interment had become an extraordinary incident involving police, social workers, almost the entire Catholic Church and, of course, the press. He could have said more about the old convent, how zoning had forced Loveridge & Co to build town houses on the site instead of motels and restaurant as planned, and he could have described the new convent, a modest three-bedroomed house close to town, and how he and Jude had tried to buy it when Sister Agnes, the last of the three, went into a nursing home. As newlyweds, they had fancied the stained glass window featuring St Joseph with his hammer and his brown apron in their bedroom. But the house had rightly gone to the parish to become a drop-in centre for the elderly.

After Christmas 1980, his visits to the Sisters became fewer and may have finished altogether but for Sister Mary Clare's sudden death in 1988, when he was in the sixth form. He and his father and Liz had taken time out to share the vigil of rejoicing with Sister Agnes and after that he'd kept regular contact with her, a new relationship based on kinship and recognition of genes shared. The holiday, which he still thought of as the time of snow, became encapsulated as the most significant experience of his childhood, more so, even, than his mother's death. He didn't know how to analyse it, for his memory held it seamless and beyond dissection. He didn't even know why he tended to classify his childhood in two parts, before snow and after snow. He was tempted to describe the holiday as the pivotal experience of his youth but those words, too, were so clichéd they could not be considered valid.

He rode over the footpath, through the smell of dog droppings and jasmine cooked together by afternoon heat, through the gate, dodging Meg's red plastic tricycle, up the driveway and into the garage. They had been fortunate to buy at auction the Holden station wagon, now twenty-five years old but with less than a hundred thousand on the clock. After that summer, it was hardly ever driven. Sister Agnes's licence was not renewed and the vehicle, serviced occasionally by Brian's father, remained in the new convent garage except for a few occasions when it was used by visiting priests or religious. He felt that Sister Luke's death in the back seat had blessed the old wagon and given it a distinction as close to canonisation as a vehicle could get. Liz agreed with him but Jude did not. Too liberal to be outraged by his opinion and too practical to be superstitious, Jude nonetheless did not like him talking about Sister Luke's passing and said he should let the matter rest in peace. He was sure that deep down she was relieved that the film was not going ahead.

He found her in the kitchen, kneeling beside Anthony, cutting bubble gum out of his hair. Meg, who had presumably put the gum in, was watching with interest, her fingers in her mouth.

Jude looked up. 'You're early.' She snipped with the scissors, a tuft as fine as a paintbrush. 'Are you okay?'

'Absolutely,' he said, shrugging off his backpack. 'Hello Meggy, hello Anthony. Gum, eh? Where did you get that?'

Anthony, a two-year-old version of Jude, rubbed his hair and laughed. 'Bubba gum. Bubba gum.'

Meg, who was all Collins down to the lean face and eyes layered with secrets, said defensively, 'It was Aunty Nicky's bubble gum. Anthony got it out of Aunty Nicky's purse.'

'You didn't sound okay when you phoned,' said Jude, flicking the matted bit of hair into the garbage. She wiped the scissors on her dress and put them back in the drawer. 'It really isn't the end of the world, you know.'

'It wasn't the rejection so much as her attitude,' he said.

'Oh?'

'Jude, she was a symptom. She reflected the malaise of the entire media in this country. Corruption is newsworthy. Goodness is irrelevant.'

'Is that what she said?' She cut an apple for the children.

'In effect, she did. We don't have a story, she said. This is not what we want, she said. Do you know what they did want? They wanted a scandal. They wanted me to write lies. This is how they shape the minds of youth and then, you know, they use the results to provide themselves with more material. The entire country is caught in a cycle of negativity engineered by the media.'

Jude gave him a warning look and he realised that he was shouting. Anthony's eyes were wide. Meg was looking wary. He went to them, picked them up in turn, kissed and tickled them. 'What are we going to do with this grumpy old Daddy?'

Meg shrieked with laughter, recognising the game. 'Make him into bread. Make him into cheese. Feed him to the ducks. Feed him to the geese.'

'Feeda duck,' echoed Anthony.

The children hung about his neck and were prised away by Jude, who gave them some apple and then came back to him, putting her arms around him. 'As long as this script business doesn't eat you up,' she said. 'That's the main thing.'

He sighed. 'I suddenly felt so insignificant,' he said, 'so second-rate.'

'What? The talented Mr Collins? Teacher? Poet? Married to a devastatingly gorgeous wife and with two beautiful children?'

'Don't patronise me, Jude. I've had enough of that.'

'Oh Brian.' She rocks against him, trying to soothe. 'You're not second-rate. You're a good teacher, and I love your poetry. Remember the lines you wrote on our first anniversary? Make love with reverence, give birth to light. Remember?'

'Oh!' he winced, drawing away from her. 'That is so tacky! I should be writing greeting cards.'

'You did write it in a card,' she said, 'and it's not tacky. Anyway, what's wrong with a little tackiness? It's cynicism I find hard to live with.'

'I'm sorry.' He hugged her and nuzzled her neck. 'I'm coping. Just give me some time.'

She was quiet for a moment, then she said, 'Do they know about Sister Agnes?'

'Dear God, no! Can you imagine it? They'd rush down to Mary Crest with their cameras, pelting her with questions.'

Jude rested her head on his shoulder. 'She didn't have a good night.'

'No?'

'They said her breathing is getting worse. They've increased her diuretics. Father Cassidy was up there this morning. He told me he'd be surprised if she lasted the week.'

He drew away from her. 'When do you plan dinner?'

'You've got an hour or more,' she said. 'Don't forget the envelope. I left it by the bed.'

* * *

His mountain bike, not three months old, was as well programmed for Mary Crest Rest Home as it was for Girls' High School and even through late afternoon traffic he could make the distance from his gate to the entrance in under seven minutes. He walked in, greeting the staff, some of whom he had known all his life, and continued on down the red-carpeted corridor lined with handrails and the occasional wheelchair.

She was propped up against pillows, looking all of her ninety-seven years but with a beauty she did not possess when she was younger. The veil had gone. She was bald save for a few wisps of white hair and her face was too thin for the lines that once gave it a severe expression. Her beauty was that of bone structure, fine skull, high cheekbones, aquiline nose, the appeal of a winter tree whose bark had become so fine it was almost transparent.

When she saw him, her eyes gathered up the light of greeting but her breathing was too laboured for anything beyond a smile. He put down his cycle helmet and sat beside the bed, placing his hand palm upwards on the white cover. Her thin mottled hand came down over his, cold and almost weightless, and he began the visit with the usual routine of parish news, little threads from the tapestry of her life's work, picked up and carried on, Tommy Blanchard diagnosed with diabetes, the Leary family buying a new fridge, the Hogan baby walking already at nine months, Molly Stratton's grandson getting honours in his music exams, these were the items he brought her two or three times a week, knowing that they were of much more value than chocolates or flowers. When the news had run its course, he usually took a volume of poetry from his jacket pocket and read to her. Yeats and Manley Hopkins were her favourites but sometimes he anonymously added one of his own poems in some kind of sentimental gesture. These days, the nursing staff called her Agnes. He never did. It was always Sister except for close moments when it was no name at all.

He withdrew his hands from hers to get the envelope. He opened it and tipped out a stalk of flowers so old that it had dried to a pale brown. He explained, 'On Saturday we took out the car seats to clean, and this is what we found. Do you recognise it? A Russell lupin.'

She looked at it without expression.

He said, 'The day before that trip to the mountain, we had lunch by a wilderness of wildflowers. Do you remember?'

She shook her head at him and her lips formed a no.

'I picked some for Sister Luke who was sitting in the front seat.'

She smiled then, and on a wheezing breath, said, 'Ah – Luke!'

'Did I ever tell you Sister Luke's last words to me? They may well have been the very last words she uttered. She told me to use a fork, not an egg beater, to make an omelette. I remembered that. As it turned out, it was very good advice which I shall no doubt pass on to my grandchildren on my deathbed.'

She was nodding, smiling, as close as she could get to laughter.

He replaced his hand under hers. 'Jude sends her love. We want to remind you that when the time comes, we will do your vigil.' He felt the pressure on his fingers. 'It's important to us,' he said.

She was breathing faster and her lips were shaping words. 'I –

want – to go – home.' She turned her head to him. 'Home – to – God.'

'I know.' He leaned forward and kissed her forehead. Then he said, 'Remember that line you used to quote from Tennyson? They also serve who only stand and wait.'

Her eyes widened and she jerked her hand on his.

'Oh,' he said. 'Was it Keats?'

Then she knew he was teasing. She smiled, wheezed and rested back on the pillow.

'I guess it must have been Milton, Sister,' he said.